The Story of the Battle Hymn of the Republic

Florence Howe Hall

Alpha Editions

This edition published in 2024

ISBN : 9789362999436

Design and Setting By
Alpha Editions
www.alphaedis.com
Email - info@alphaedis.com

As per information held with us this book is in Public Domain.
This book is a reproduction of an important historical work. Alpha Editions uses the best technology to reproduce historical work in the same manner it was first published to preserve its original nature. Any marks or number seen are left intentionally to preserve its true form.

Contents

I THE ANTI-SLAVERY PRELUDE TO THE GREAT TRAGEDY OF THE CIVIL WAR ......- 1 -

II THE CRIME AGAINST KANSAS ......- 9 -

III MRS. HOWE VISITS THE ARMY OF THE POTOMAC ......- 17 -

IV "THE BATTLE HYMN OF THE REPUBLIC" ......- 22 -

V THE ARMY TAKES IT UP ......- 29 -

VI NOTABLE OCCASIONS WHERE IT HAS BEEN SUNG ......- 33 -

VII HOW AND WHERE THE AUTHOR RECITED IT ......- 40 -

VIII TRIBUTES TO "THE BATTLE HYMN" ......- 44 -

IX MRS. HOWE'S LESSER POEMS OF THE CIVIL WAR ......- 50 -

X MRS. HOWE'S LOVE OF FREEDOM AN INHERITANCE ......- 59 -

FOOTNOTES: ......- 64 -

I
THE ANTI-SLAVERY PRELUDE TO THE GREAT TRAGEDY OF THE CIVIL WAR

The encroachments of the slave power on Northern soil—Green Peace, the home of Julia Ward Howe, a center of anti-slavery activity—She assists her husband, Dr. Samuel Gridley Howe, in editing the *Commonwealth*—He is made chairman of the Vigilance Committee—Slave concealed at Green Peace—Charles Sumner is struck down in the United States Senate.

THE "Battle Hymn of the Republic," "the crimson flower of battle," bloomed in a single night. It sprang from the very soil of the conflict, in the midst of the Civil War. Yet the plant which produced it was of slow growth, with roots reaching far back into the past.

In order to understand how this song of our nation sprang into sudden being we must study that stormy past—the prelude of the Civil War. How greatly it affected my mother we shall see from her own record, as well as from the story of the events that touched her so nearly. My own memory of them dates back to childhood's days. Yet they moved and stirred my soul as few things have done in a long life.

Therefore I have striven to give to the present generation some idea of the fervor and ferment, the exaltation of spirit, that prevailed at that epoch among the soldiers of a great cause, especially as I saw it in our household.

Let the Hero, born of woman, crush the serpent with his heel.

So many years have elapsed since the evil monster of slavery was done to death that we sometimes forget its awful power in the middle of the last century. The fathers of the Republic believed that it would soon perish. They forbade its entrance into the Territories and were careful to make no mention of it in the Constitution.

The invention of the cotton-gin changed the whole situation. It was found that slave labor could be used with profit in the cultivation of the cotton crop. But slave labor with its wasteful methods exhausted the soil. Slavery could only be made profitable by constantly increasing its area. Hence, the Southern leaders departed from the policy of the fathers of the Republic. Instead of allowing slavery to die out, they determined to make it perpetual.

Instead of keeping it within the limits prescribed by the ancient law of the land, they resolved to extend it.

The Missouri Compromise of 1820 gave the first extension of slavery, opening the great Territory of Missouri to the embrace of the serpent. The fugitive-slave law was signed in 1850. Before this time the return of runaway negroes had been an uncertain obligation. The new law took away from State magistrates the decision in cases of this sort and gave it to United States Commissioners. It imposed penalties on rescues and denied a jury trial to black men arrested as fugitives, thus greatly endangering the liberties of free negroes. The Dred Scott decision (see page 10), denying that negroes could be citizens, was made in 1854. In 1856 the Missouri Compromise was repealed by the Kansas and Nebraska law.[1] Additional territory was thrown open to the sinister institution which now threatened to become like the great Midgard snake, holding our country in its suffocating embrace, as that creature of fable surrounded the earth. It was necessary to fling off the deadly coils of slavery if we were to endure as a free nation.

The first step was to arouse the sleeping conscience of the people. For the South was not alone in wishing there should be no interference with their "peculiar institution." The North was long supine and dreaded any new movement that might interfere with trade and national prosperity. I can well remember my father's pointing this out to his children, and inveighing against the selfishness of the merchants as a class. Alas! it was a Northern man, Stephen A. Douglas, who was the father of the Kansas and Nebraska bill.

"The trumpet note of Garrison" had sounded, some years before this time, the first note of anti-slavery protest. But the Garrisonian abolitionists did not seek to carry the question into politics. Indeed, they held it to be wrong to vote under the Federal Constitution, "A league with death and a covenant with hell," as they called it. Whittier, the Quaker poet, took a more practical view than his fellow-abolitionists and advocated the use of the ballot-box.

When the encroachments of the slave power began to threaten seriously free institutions throughout the country, thinking men at the North saw that the time for political action had come. There were several early organizations which preceded the formation of the Republican party—the Liberty party, Conscience Whigs, Free-soilers, as they were called. My father belonged to the two latter, and I can well remember that my elder sister and I were nicknamed at school, "Little Free-Dirters."

The election of Charles Sumner to the United States Senate was an important victory for the anti-slavery men. Dr. Howe, as his most intimate friend, worked hard to secure it. Yet we see by my father's letters that he groaned in spirit at the necessity of the political dickering which he hated.

Women in those days neither spoke in public nor took part in political affairs. But it may be guessed that my mother was deeply interested in all that was going on in the world of affairs, and under her own roof, too, for our house at South Boston became one of the centers of activity of the anti-slavery agitation.

My father (who was some seventeen years older than his wife) well understood the power of the press. He had employed it to good effect in his work for the blind, the insane, and others. Hence he became actively interested in the management of the *Commonwealth*, an anti-slavery newspaper, and with my mother's help edited it for an entire winter. They began work together every morning, he preparing the political articles, and she the literary ones. Burning words were sent forth from the quiet precincts of "Green Peace." My mother had thus named the homestead, lying in its lovely garden, when she came there early in her married life. Little did she then dream that the repeal of the Missouri Compromise would disturb its serene repose some ten years later.

The agitation had not yet become so strong as greatly to affect the children of the household. We played about the garden as usual and knew little of the *Commonwealth* undertaking, save as it brought some delightful juveniles to the editorial sanctum. The little Howes highly approved of this by-product of journalism!

Our mother's pen had been used before this time to help the cause of the slave. As early as 1848 she contributed a poem to *The Liberty Bell*, an annual edited by Mrs. Maria Norton Chapman and sold at the anti-slavery bazars. "In my first published volume, *Passion Flowers*, appeared some lines 'On the Death of the Slave Lewis,' which were wrung from my indignant heart by a story—alas! too common in those days—of murderous outrage committed by a master against his human chattel" (*Recollections of the Anti-Slavery Struggle*, Julia Ward Howe).

Another method of arousing the conscience of the nation was through the public platform. My father and his friends were anxious to present the great question in a perfectly fair way. So a series of lectures was given in Tremont Temple, where the speakers were alternately the most prominent advocates of slavery at the South and its most strenuous opponents at the North. Senator Toombs, of Georgia, and General Houston, of Texas, were among the former.

It was, probably, at this lecture course that my father exercised his office as chairman in an unusual way. In those days it was the custom to open the meeting with prayer, and some of the contemporary clergymen were very long-winded.[10] Dr. Howe informed each reverend gentleman beforehand that at the end of five minutes he should pull the latter's coat-tail. The divines were in such dread of this gentle admonition that they invariably wound up the prayer within the allotted time.

At this time no criticism of the "peculiar institution" was allowed at the South. Northerners traveling there were often asked for their opinion of it, but any unfavorable comment evoked displeasure. Indeed, a friend of ours, a Northern woman teaching in Louisiana, was called to book because in his presence she spoke of one of the slaves as a "man." A negro, she was informed, was not a man, and must never be so called. "Boy" was the proper term to use. This was a logical inference from Judge Taney's famous Dred Scott decision—*viz.*, that "such persons," *i. e.*, negroes, "were not included among the people" in the words of the Declaration of Independence, and could not in any respect be considered as citizens. Yet, to quote Abraham Lincoln again, "Judge Curtis, in his dissenting opinion, shows that in five of the then thirteen States—to wit, New Hampshire, Massachusetts, New York, New Jersey, and North Carolina—free negroes were voters, and in[11] proportion to their numbers had the same part in making the Constitution that the white people had."

Events now began to move with ever-increasing rapidity. The scenes of the stirring prelude to the Civil War grew ever more stormy. Men became more and more wrought up as the relentless purpose of the Southern leaders was gradually revealed. The deadly serpent of slavery became a hydra-headed monster, striking north, east, and west. The hunting of fugitive slaves took on a sinister activity in the Northern "border" States; at the national capital the attempts to muzzle free speech culminated in the striking down of Charles Sumner in the Senate Chamber itself; in Kansas the "border ruffians" strove to inaugurate a reign of terror, and succeeded in bringing on a local conflict which was the true opening of the Civil War.

The men who combated the dragon of slavery—the Siegfrieds of that day—fought him in all these directions. In Boston Dr. Howe was among the first to organize resistance to the rendition of fugitive slaves. An escaped negro was kidnapped there in 1846. This was four years before the passage by Congress of the fugitive-slave law made[12] it the duty (!) of the Free States to return runaway negroes to slavery. My father called a meeting of protest at Faneuil Hall. He was the chief speaker and "every sentence was a sword-thrust" (T. W. Higginson's account). I give a brief extract from his address:

"The peculiar institution which has so long been brooding over the country like an incubus has at length spread abroad its murky wings and has covered us with its benumbing shadow. It has silenced the pulpit, it has muffled the press; its influence is everywhere.... Court Street can find no way of escape for the poor slave. State Street, that drank the blood of the martyrs of liberty—State Street is deaf to the cry of the oppressed slave; the port of Boston that has been shut up by a tyrant king as the dangerous haunt of free-men—the port of Boston has been opened to the slave-trader; for God's sake, Mr. Chairman, let us keep Faneuil Hall free!"

Charles Sumner, Wendell Phillips, and Theodore Parker also spoke. John Quincy Adams presided at the meeting.

The meeting resulted in the formation of a vigilance committee of forty, with my father as chairman. This continued its work until the[13] hunting of fugitives ceased in Boston. Secrecy necessarily characterized its proceedings. An undated note from Dr. Howe to Theodore Parker gives us a hint of them:

[2]DEAR T. P.—Write me a note by bearer. Tell him merely whether I am wanted to-night; if I am he will act accordingly about bringing my wagon.

I could bring any one here and keep him secret a week and no person except Mrs. H. and myself would know it.

Yours,

CHEV.[3]

This letter raises an interesting question. Were fugitives concealed, unknown to us children, in our house? It is quite possible, for both our parents could keep a secret. I remember a young white girl who was so hidden from her drunken father until other arrangements could be made for her. I remember also a negro girl, hardly more than a child, who was secreted beneath the roof of Green Peace. Her mistress had brought her to Boston as a servant. Since she was not a runaway, the provisions of the odious fugitive-slave law did not apply to her. Here at least we could cry:

No fetters in the Bay State!

No slave upon her land!

My father applied to the courts and in due process of time Martha was declared free—so long as she remained on Northern soil. It may be guessed that she did not care to return to the South!

The feeling of the community was strongly opposed to taking part in slave-hunts. Yankee ingenuity often found a way to escape this odious task, and yet keep within the letter of the law.

A certain United States marshal thus explained his proceedings:

"Why, I never have any trouble about runaway slaves. If I hear that one has come to Boston I just go up to Nigger Hill [a part of Joy Street] and say to them, 'Do you know of any runaway slaves about here?' And they never do!"

This was a somewhat unique way of giving notice to the friends of the fugitive that the officers of the law were after him.

If he could only escape over the border into free Canada he was safe. According to the English law no slave could remain such on British soil. The moment he "shook the Lion's paw" he became free. Our law in these United States is founded on the English Common Law. Alas! the pro-slavery party succeeded in overthrowing it. No wonder that Senator Toombs, of Georgia, boasted that he would call the roll of his slaves under the shadow of Bunker Hill Monument. The fugitive-slave law gave him the power to do this, and thus make our boasted freedom of the soil only an empty mockery.

The vigilance committee did its work well, and for some time no runaway slaves were captured in Boston. One poor wretch was finally caught. My mother thus describes the event:

"At last a colored fugitive, Anthony Burns by name, was captured and held subject to the demands of his owner. The day of his rendition was a memorable one in Boston. The courthouse was surrounded by chains and guarded with cannon. The streets were thronged with angry faces. Emblems of mourning hung from several business and newspaper offices. With a show of military force the fugitive was marched through the streets. No rescue was attempted at this time, although one had been planned for an earlier date. The ordinance was executed; Burns was delivered to his master. But the act once consummated in broad daylight could never be repeated" (from Julia Ward Howe's *Recollections of the Anti-Slavery Struggle*).

So great was the public indignation against the judge who had allowed himself to be the instrument of the Federal Government in the return of Burns to slavery that he was removed from office. Shortly afterward he left Boston and went to live in Washington.

The attempts to enforce the fugitive-slave law at the East failed, as they were bound to fail. The efforts to muzzle free speech at the national capital were more successful for a time.

The task of Charles Sumner in upholding the principles of freedom in the United States Senate was colossal. For long he stood almost alone, "A voice crying in the wilderness, make straight the paths of the Lord." Fortunately he was endowed by nature with a commanding figure and presence and a wonderful voice that fitted him perfectly for his great task. My mother thus described him:

"He was majestic in person, habitually reserved and rather distant in manner, but sometimes unbent to a smile in which the real geniality of his soul seemed to shed itself abroad. His voice was ringing and melodious, his gestures somewhat constrained, his whole manner, like his matter, weighty and full of dignity."

As an old and intimate friend, my father sometimes urged him to greater haste in his task of combating slavery at the national capital. Thus Charles Sumner writes to him from Washington, February 1, 1854:

DEAR HOWE—Do not be impatient with me. I am doing all that I can. This great wickedness disturbs my sleep, my rest, my appetite. Much is to be done, of which the world knows nothing, in rallying an opposition. It has been said by others, that but for Chase and Sumner this Bill would have been rushed through at once, even without debate. Douglas himself told me that our opposition was the only sincere opposition he had to encounter. But this is not true. There are others here who are in earnest.

My longing is to rally the country against the Bill[4] and I desire to let others come forward and broaden our front.

Our Legislature ought to speak *unanimously*. Our people should revive the old report and resolutions of 1820.[5]

At present our first wish is delay, that the country may be aroused.

"Would that night or Blücher had come!"

God bless you always!

C. S.

In the fateful spring of 1856 Dr. and Mrs. Howe were in Washington. They saw both Charles Sumner and Preston Brooks. My mother has given us pictures of the two men as she then saw them:

"Charles Sumner looked up and, seeing me in the gallery, greeted me with a smile of recognition. I shall never forget the beauty of that smile. It seemed to me to illuminate the whole precinct with a silvery radiance. There was in it all the innocence of his sweet and noble nature."[6]

"At Willard's Hotel I observed at a table near our own a typical Southerner of that time, handsome, but with a reckless and defiant expression of countenance which struck me unpleasantly. This was Preston Brooks, of South Carolina."[7]

During one of his visits to the Howes, Sumner said:

"I shall soon deliver a speech in the Senate which will occasion a good deal of excitement. It will not surprise me if people leave their seats and show signs of unusual disturbance."

My mother comments thus:

"At the moment I did not give much heed to his words, but they came back to me, not much later, with the force of prophecy. For Mr. Sumner did make this speech, and though at the moment nothing was done against him, the would-be assassin only waited for a more convenient season to spring upon his victim and to maim him for life. Choosing a moment when Mr. Sumner's immediate friends were not in the Senate Chamber, Brooks of South Carolina, armed with a cane of india-rubber, attacked him in the rear, knocking him from his seat with one blow, and beating him about the head until he lay bleeding and senseless upon the floor. Although the partisans of the South openly applauded this deed, its cowardly brutality was really repudiated by all who had any sense of honor, without geographical distinction. The blow, fatal to Sumner's health, was still more fatal to the cause it was meant to serve, and even to the man who dealt it. Within one year his murderous hand was paralyzed in death, and Sumner, after hanging long between life and death, stood once more erect, with the aureole of martyrdom on his brow, and with the dear-bought glory of his scars a more potent witness for the truth than ever. His place in the Senate remained for a time eloquently empty."[8]

Hon. Miles Taylor, of Louisiana, defended in the Senate the attack on Sumner. A part of his speech makes curious reading:

"If this new dogma" (the evil of slavery) "should be received by the American people with favor, it can only be when all respect for revelation ... has been utterly swept away by such a flood of irreligion and foul philosophy as never before set in."

II
THE CRIME AGAINST KANSAS

Border ruffians from Missouri carry Kansas elections with pistol and bowie-knife. They prevent peaceable Free State emigrants from entering the national territory—Dr. Howe carries out aid from New England—Clergymen and Sharp's rifles—Mrs. Howe's indignant verses—She opens the door for John Brown, the hero of the war in Kansas—Gov. Andrew, Theodore Parker, Charles Sumner—The attack on Fort Sumter—"The death-blow of slavery."

THESE assaults by the serpent of slavery on the free institutions of the North and East were dangerous enough, yet, like other evils, they brought their own remedies with them. Such an open attack on free speech as that on Sumner was sure to be resented, while the forcible carrying-off of fugitive slaves under the shadow of old Faneuil Hall aroused a degree of wrath that even the pro-slavery leaders saw was ominous.

"The crime against Kansas" was still more alarming because it threatened to turn a free Territory into a slave State. In 1854 the Kansas and Nebraska bill had been passed, repealing the Missouri Compromise and exposing a vast area of virgin soil to the encroachments of the "peculiar institution."

The Free-soil men were speedily on the alert. During that same year of 1854 two Massachusetts colonies were sent out to Kansas, others going later.

But the leaders of the slave power had no intention of allowing men from the free States to settle peacefully in Kansas. They had repealed the Missouri Compromise with the express purpose of gaining a new slave State, and this was to be accomplished by whatever means were necessary.

It was an easy matter to send men from Missouri into the adjacent Territory of Kansas—to vote there and then to return to their homes across the Mississippi.

The New York *Herald* of April 20, 1855, published the following letter from a correspondent in Brunswick, Missouri:

From five to seven thousand men started from Missouri to attend the election, some to remove, but the most to return to their families, with an intention, if they liked the Territory, to make it their permanent abode at the earliest moment practicable. But they intended to vote.... Indeed, every county furnished its quota; and when they set out it looked like an army.... They were armed.... Fifteen hundred wore on their hats bunches of hemp. They were resolved if a tyrant attempted to trample upon the rights of the sovereign people to hang him.

It will be noted that "the rights of the sovereign people" were to go to the ballot-box not in their own, but in another State. These "border ruffians" took possession of the polls and carried the first election with pistol and bowie-knife.

The pro-slavery leaders strove to drive out the colonists from the free States and to prevent additional emigrants from entering the Territory. A campaign of frightfulness was inaugurated—with the usual result.

Governor Geary of Kansas, although a pro-slavery official himself, wrote (Dec. 22, 1856) that he heartily despised the abolitionists, but that *"The persecutions of the Free State men here were not exceeded by those of the early Christians."*

My father was deeply interested in the colonization of Kansas and in the struggle for freedom within its borders. He helped in 1854 to organize the "New England Emigrant Aid Company" which assisted parties of settlers to go to the Territory. In 1856 matters began to look very dark for the colonists from the free States. "Dr. Howe was stirred to his highest activity by the news from Kansas and by the brutal assault on Charles Sumner" (F. B. Sanborn). With others he called and organized the Faneuil Hall meeting. He was made chairman of its committee, and at once sent two thousand dollars to St. Louis for use in Kansas. This prompt action had an important effect on the discouraged settlers. Soon afterward he started for Kansas to give further aid to the colonists.

"I have traversed the whole length of the State of Iowa on horseback or in a cart, sleeping in said cart or in worse lodgings, among dirty men on the floor of dirty huts. We have organized a pretty good line of communication between our base and the corps of emigrants who have now advanced into the Territory of Nebraska. Everything depends upon the success of the attempt to break through the *cordon infernale* which Missouri has drawn across the northern frontier of Kansas."[9]

In another letter he writes:

The boats on the river are beset by spies and ruffians, are hauled up at various places and thoroughly searched for anti-slavery men.

He thus describes the emigrants:[10]

CAMP OF THE EMIGRATION, NEBRASKA TERRITORY,
July 29, '56.

The emigration is indeed a noble one; sturdy, industrious, temperate, resolute men.... I wish our friends in the East could know the character and behavior of these emigrants. They are and have been for two weeks encamped out upon these vast prairies in their tents and waggons waiting patiently for the signal to move, exhausting all peaceful resources and negotiations before resorting to force.

There is no liquor in the whole camp; no smoking, no swearing, no irregularity. They drink cold water, live mostly on mush and rice and the simplest, cheapest fare. They have instruction for the little children; they have Sunday-schools, prayer-meetings, and are altogether a most sober and earnest community. Most of the loafers have dropped off. The Wisconsin company, about one hundred, give a tone to all the others. I could give you a picture of the drunken, rollicking ruffians who oppose this emigration—but you know it. Will the North allow such an emigration to be shut out of the National Territory by such brigands?

In another letter he tells us that among the emigrants were thirty-eight women and children—grandfathers and grandmothers, too, journeying with their live stock in carts drawn by oxen to the promised land.

He says nothing of danger to himself, but Hon. Andrew D. White tells us that "Dr. Howe had braved death again and again while aiding the Free State men against the pro-slavery myrmidons of Kansas."

The strength of the movement may be judged from the fact that during this year (1856) the people of Massachusetts sent one hundred thousand dollars in money, clothing, and arms to help the Free State colonists. This money did not come from the radicals only, but from "Hunkers," as they were then called—*i. e.*, conservative and well-to-do citizens. My father wrote: "People pay readily here for Sharp's rifles. One lady offered me one hundred dollars the other day, and to-day a clergyman offered me one hundred dollars."

My mother was greatly moved by these tragic events—the assault on Sumner and the civil war in Kansas. In *Words for the Hour*—a volume of her poems published in 1857—we find a record of her just indignation. In the "Sermon of Spring" she describes Kansas as:

Wearing the green nodding plumes of the Court of the Prairie,

Gyves on her free-born limbs, on her fair arms shackles,

Blood on her garments, terror and grief in her features.

"Tremble," she cried, "tho' the battle seem thine for a season,

Not a drop of my blood shall be wanting to judge thee.

Tremble, thou fallen from mercy ere fallen from office."

This poem, which is a long one, contains a tribute to Sumner, as do also "Tremont Temple," "The Senator's Return," and "An Hour in the Senate." I give a brief extract from the last named:

Falls there no lightning from yon distant heaven

To crush this man's potential impudence?

Shall not its outraged patience thunder: "Hence!

Forsake the shrine where Liberty was given!"

"The strong shall rule, the arm of force have sway,

The helpless multitude in bonds abide—"

Again the chuckle and the shake of pride—

"God's for the stronger—so great Captains say."

Yet, rise to answer, chafing in thy chair,

With soul indignant stirred, and flushing brow.

Thou art God's candidate—speak soothly now,

Let every word anticipate a prayer.

Gather in thine the outstretched hands that strive

To help thy pleading, agonized and dumb;

Bear up the hearts whose silent sorrows come

For utterance, to the voice that thou canst give.

In the same volume are verses entitled "Slave Eloquence" and "Slave Suicide."

How did the children of the household feel during this period of "Sturm und Drang"? To the older ones, at least, it was a most exciting time. While we did not by any means know of all that was going on, we felt very strongly the electric current of indignation that thrilled through our home, as well as the stir of action. My father early taught us to love freedom and to hate slavery. He gave us, in brief, clear outline, the story of the aggressions of the slave power. We knew of the iniquity of the Dred Scott decision before we were in our teens. Child that I was, I was greatly moved when he repeated Lowell's well-known lines:

Truth forever on the scaffold, Wrong forever on the throne,—

Yet that scaffold sways the future, and, behind the dim unknown,

Standeth God within the shadow, keeping watch above His own.

My father had always something of the soldier about him—a quick, active step, gallant bearing, and a voice tender, yet strong, "A voice to lead a regiment." This was the natural consequence of his early experiences in the Greek War of Independence, when he served some seven years as surgeon, soldier, and—most important of all—almoner of America's bounty to the peaceful population. The latter would have perished of starvation save for the supplies sent out in response to Dr. Howe's appeals to his countrymen. The greater part of his life was devoted to the healing arts of the good physician. Yet the portraits of him, taken during the tremendous struggle of the anti-slavery period, show a sternness not visible in his younger nor yet in his later days.

In her poem "A Rough Sketch" my mother described him as he seemed to her at this time:

A great grieved heart, an iron will,

As fearless blood as ever ran;

A form elate with nervous strength

And fibrous vigor,—all a man.

Charles Sumner came often to Green Peace when he was in Boston. We children greatly admired him. He seemed to us, and doubtless to others, a species of superman. I can hardly think of those days without the organ accompaniment of his voice—deeper than the depths, round and full. When our friend was stricken down in the Senate, great was our youthful indignation. Many were the arguments held with our mates at school and dancing-school, often the children of the "Hunker" class. They sought to justify the attack, and we replied with the testimony of an eye-witness to the scene (Henry Wilson, afterward Vice-President of the United States) and the fact that a colleague of Brooks stood, waving a pistol[11] in each hand, to prevent any interference in behalf of Sumner. We had heard about the cruel "Mochsa" with which his back was burned in the hope of cure, and we lamented his sufferings.

John A. Andrew, afterward the War Governor of the State, was another intimate of our household, a great friend of both our parents. Genial and merry, as a rule, he yet could be sternly eloquent in the denunciation of slavery.

Indeed, it was a speech of this nature which first brought him into prominence. In the Massachusetts Legislature of 1858 the most striking figure was that of Caleb Cushing. He had been Attorney-General in President Franklin Pierce's Cabinet and was one of the ablest lawyers in the United States. When all were silent before his oratory and no one felt equal to opposing this master of debate, Andrew, a young advocate, was moved, like another David, to attack his Goliath. In a speech of great eloquence he vindicated the action of the Governor and the Legislature in removing from office the judge who had sent Anthony Burns back into slavery and thus outraged the conscience of the Bay State. As a lawyer he sustained his opinion by legal precedents.

"When he took his seat there was a storm of applause. The House was wild with excitement. Some members cried for joy; others cheered, waved their handkerchiefs, and threw whatever they could find into the air."[12]

And so, like David, he won not only the battle of the day, but the leadership of his people in the stormy times that soon followed.

When a box of copperhead snakes was sent to our beloved Governor we were again indignant. (Political opponents had not then learned to send gifts of bombs.)

From Kansas itself Martin F. Conway came to us, full of fiery zeal for the Free State cause, although born south of Mason and Dixon's line.

He later represented the young State in Congress. Samuel Downer and George L. Stearns we often saw; both were very active in the anti-slavery cause. The latter was remarkable for a very long and beautiful beard, brown and soft, like a woman's hair and reaching to his waist.

We heard burning words about the duty of Massachusetts during these assaults of the slave power. Could she endure them, or should she not rather seek to withdraw from the Union?

These words sound strangely to us now, but it must be remembered that in the fifties we had seen our fair Bay State made an annex to slave territory. Men might well ask one another, "Can the Commonwealth of Massachusetts endure the disgrace of having slave-hunts within her borders?" "The Irrepressible Conflict" had come. When the pro-slavery leaders forced the fugitive-slave law through Congress they struck a blow at the life of the nation as deadly as that of Fort Sumter. The latter was the inevitable sequel of the former.

We saw often at Green Peace another intimate friend of our parents—Theodore Parker, the famous preacher and reformer. As he wore spectacles and was prematurely bald, he did not leave upon our childish minds the impression of grandeur inseparably connected with Charles Sumner. Yet the splendid dome of his head gave evidence of his great intellect, while his blue eyes looked kindly and often merrily at us. Having no children of his own, he would have liked to adopt our youngest sister, could our parents have been persuaded to part with her.

Theodore Parker advocated the anti-slavery cause with great eloquence in the pulpit. He also belonged to my father's vigilance committee and harbored fugitive slaves in his own home. To one couple of runaway negroes he presented a Bible and a sword—after marrying them legally—a thing not always done in the day of slavery. My father succeeded in sending away from Boston the man who attempted to carry them back to the South, and William and Ellen Croft found freedom in England.

Theodore Parker's sermons had a powerful influence on his great congregation, of which my mother was for some time a member. In one of her tributes to him she tells us how he drew them all toward the light of a better day and prepared them also for "the war of blood and iron."

"I found that it was by the spirit of the higher humanity that he brought his hearers into sympathy with all reforms and with the better society that should ripen out of them. Freedom for black and white, opportunity for man and woman, the logic of conscience and the logic of progress—this was the discipline of his pulpit.... Before its [the Civil War's] first trumpet blast blew his great heart had ceased to beat. But a great body of us remembered his prophecy and his strategy and might have cried, as did Walt Whitman at a later date, 'O captain, my captain!'"[13]

Rev. James Freeman Clarke, our pastor for many years, was among those whose visits gave pleasure and inspiration as well to our household. He did not hesitate to preach anti-slavery doctrines, unpopular as they were, from his pulpit. My mother says of him at this time:

"In the agitated period which preceded the Civil War and in that which followed it he in his modest pulpit became one of the leaders, not of his own flock alone, but of the community to which he belonged. I can imagine few things more instructive and desirable than was his preaching in those troublous times, so full of unanswered question and unreconciled discord."[14] Her beloved minister was among those who accompanied my mother on the visit to the army which inspired "The Battle Hymn of the Republic." This was written to the tune of:

John Brown's body lies a-moldering in the grave,

His soul is marching on.

"Old Ossawotamie Brown" was the true hero of the bloody little war in Kansas, where the Free State men finally prevailed, though many lives were lost. He has been called "Savior of Kansas and Liberator of the Slave." He came at least once to Green Peace. My mother has described her meeting with him. My father had told her some time previously about a man who "seemed to intend to devote his life to the redemption of the colored race from slavery, even as Christ had willingly offered His life for the salvation of mankind." One day he reminded her of the person so described, and added: "That man will call here this afternoon. You will receive him. His name is John Brown."...

Later, my mother wrote of this meeting:

"At the expected time I heard the bell ring, and, on answering it, beheld a middle-aged, middle-sized man, with hair and beard of amber color streaked with gray. He looked a Puritan of the Puritans, forceful, concentrated, and self-contained. We had a brief interview, of which I only remember my great gratification at meeting one of whom I had heard so good an account. I saw him once again at Dr. Howe's office, and then heard no more of him for some time."[15] Elsewhere she has written apropos of his raid at Harper's Ferry:

"None of us could exactly approve an act so revolutionary in its character, yet the great-hearted attempt enlisted our sympathies very strongly. The weeks of John Brown's imprisonment were very sad ones, and the day of his death was one of general mourning in New England."[16]

With the election of Lincoln we seemed to come to smoother times. We young people certainly did not realize that we were on the brink of civil war, although friends who had visited the South warned us of the preparations going on there. If there should be any struggle, it would be a brief one, people said. Suddenly, like a flash of lightning out of a clear sky, came the firing on Sumter. My father came triumphantly into the nursery and called out to his children: "Sumter has been fired upon! That's the death-blow of slavery." Little did he or we realize how long and terrible the conflict would be. But he knew that the serpent had received its death-wound. All through the long and terrible war he cheered my mother by his unyielding belief in the ultimate success of our arms. So the prelude ended and the greater tragedy began. The conflict of ideas, the most soul-stirring period of our history, passed into the conflict of arms. In the midst of its agony the steadfast soul of a woman saw the presage of victory and gave the message, a message never to be forgotten, to her people and to the world.

III
MRS. HOWE VISITS THE ARMY OF THE POTOMAC

The Civil War breaks out—Dr. Howe is appointed a member of the Sanitary Commission—Mrs. Howe accompanies him to Washington—She makes her maiden speech to a Massachusetts regiment—She sees the watch-fires of a hundred circling camps—She visits the army and her carriage is involved in a military movement—She is surrounded by "Burnished rows of steel."

"THE years between 1850 and 1857, eventful as they were, appear to me almost a period of play when compared with the time of trial which was to follow. It might have been likened to the tuning of instruments before some great musical solemnity. The theme was already suggested, but of its wild and terrible development who could have had any foreknowledge?"

In her *Reminiscences* my mother thus compares the Civil War and its prelude. Again she says of the former:

"Its cruel fangs fastened upon the very heart of Boston and took from us our best and bravest. From many a stately mansion father or son went forth, followed by weeping, to be brought back for bitterer sorrow."

Mercifully she was spared this last. My father was too old for military service and no longer in vigorous health, being in his sixtieth year when the war broke out; my eldest brother was just thirteen years of age. Nevertheless she was brought into close touch with the activities of the great struggle from the beginning.

On the day when the news of the attack on Fort Sumter was received Dr. Howe wrote to Governor Andrew, offering his services:

"Since they will have it so—in the name of God, Amen! Now let all the governors and chief men of the people see to it that war shall not cease until emancipation is secure. If I can be of any use, anywhere, in any capacity (save that of spy), command me."[17]

With what swiftness the "Great War Governor of Massachusetts" acted at this time is matter of history. Two days after the President issued a call for troops, three regiments started for Washington. Massachusetts was thus the first State to come to the aid of the Union—the first, alas! to have her sons struck down and slain.

Governor Andrew was glad to avail himself of Dr. Howe's offer of aid. The latter's early experiences in Greece made his help and counsel valuable both to the State and to the nation. Gen. Winfield Scott, Commander-in-Chief of the Army, and Governor Andrew requested him, on May 2, 1861, to make a sanitary survey of the Massachusetts troops in the field at and near the national capital. Before the end of the month the Sanitary Commission was created, Dr. Howe being one of the original members appointed by Abraham Lincoln.

Governor Andrew was almost overwhelmed with the manifold cares and duties of his office. Our house was one of the places where he took refuge when he greatly needed rest. He was obliged to give up going to church early in the war because many people followed him there, importuning him with requests of all sorts.

Thus the questions of the Civil War were brought urgently to my mother's mind in her own home, just as those of the anti-slavery period had been a year or two before.

To quote her *Reminiscences* again:

"The record of our State during the war was a proud one. The repeated calls for men and for money were always promptly and generously answered. And this promptness was greatly forwarded by the energy and patriotic vigilance of the Governor. I heard much of this at the time, especially from my husband, who was greatly attached to the Governor and who himself took an intense interest in all the operations of the war.... I seemed to live in and along with the war, while it was in progress, and to follow all its ups and downs, its good and ill fortune with these two brave men, Dr. Howe and Governor Andrew. Neither of them for a moment doubted the final result of the struggle, but both they and I were often very sad and much discouraged."

Governor Andrew was often summoned to Washington. Dr. Howe's duties as a member of the Sanitary Commission also took him there. Thus it happened that my mother went to the national capital in their company in the late autumn of 1861. Mrs. Andrew, the Governor's wife, Rev. James Freeman Clarke, and Mr. and Mrs. Edwin P. Whipple were also of the party.

As they drew near Washington they saw ominous signs of the dangers encompassing the city. Mrs. Howe noticed little groups of armed men sitting near a fire—pickets guarding the railroad, her husband told her. For the Confederate Army was not far off, the Army of the Potomac lying like a steel girdle about Washington, to protect it.

This was my mother's first glimpse of the Union Army which later made such a deep impression upon her mind and heart. I have always fancied, though she does not say so, that some of the vivid images of the "Battle Hymn" were suggested by the scenes of this journey.

I have seen Him in the watch-fires of a hundred circling camps;

They have built Him an altar in the evening dews and damps;

I can read His righteous sentence by the dim and flaring lamps.

His day is marching on!

Arrived at Washington, the party established themselves at Willard's Hotel. Evidences of the war were to be seen on all sides. Soldiers on horseback galloped about the streets, while ambulances with four horses passed by the windows and sometimes stopped before the hotel itself. Near at hand, my mother saw "The ghastly advertisement of an agency for embalming and forwarding the bodies of those who had fallen in the fight or who had perished by fever."[18] In the vicinity of this establishment was the office of the New York *Herald*.

Governor Andrew and Dr. Howe were busy with their official duties; indeed, the former was under such a tremendous pressure of work and care that he died soon after the close of the war. The latter "carried his restless energy and indomitable will from camp to hospital, from battle-field to bureau." His reports and letters show how deeply he was troubled by the lack of proper sanitation among the troops.

My mother again came in touch with the Army, visiting the camps and hospitals in the company of Mr. Clarke and the Rev. William Henry Channing. It need hardly be said that these excursions were made in no spirit of idle curiosity.

In ordinary times she would not look at a cut finger if she could help it. I remember her telling us of one dreadful woman who asked to be shown the worst wound in the hospital. As a result this morbid person was so overcome with the horror of it that the surgeon was obliged to leave his patient and attend to the visitor, while she went from one fainting fit into another!

Up to this time my mother had never spoken in public. It was from the Army of the Potomac that she first received the inspiration to do so. In company with her party of friends she had made "a reconnoitering expedition," visiting, among other places, the headquarters of Col. William B. Greene, of the First Massachusetts Heavy Artillery. The colonel, who was an old friend, warmly welcomed his visitors. Soon he said to my mother, "Mrs. Howe, you must speak to my men." What did he see in her face that prompted him to make such a startling request?

It must be remembered that in 1861 the women of our country were, with some notable exceptions, entirely unaccustomed to speaking in public. A few suffragists and anti-slavery leaders addressed audiences, but my mother had not at this time joined their ranks.

Yet she doubtless then possessed, although she did not know it, the power of thus expressing herself. Colonel Greene must have read in her face something of the emotion which poured itself out in the "Battle Hymn." He must have known, too, that she had already written stirring verses. So he not only asked, but insisted that she should address the men under his command.

"Feeling my utter inability to do this, I ran away and tried to hide myself in one of the hospital tents. Colonel Greene twice found me and brought me back to his piazza, where at last I stood and told as well as I could how glad I was to meet the brave defenders of our cause and how constantly they were in my thoughts."[19]

I fear there is no record of this, her maiden speech.

Throughout her long life church-going was a comfort, one might almost say a delight, to her. During this visit to Washington, where the weeks brought so many sad sights, she had the pleasure of listening on Sunday to the Rev. William Henry Channing. Love of his native land induced him to leave his pulpit in England and to return to this country in her hour of darkness and danger.

My mother tells us that this nephew of the great Dr. Channing was heir to the latter's spiritual distinction and deeply stirred by enthusiasm in a noble cause. "On Sundays his voice rang out, clear and musical as a bell, within the walls of the Unitarian church"[20]—her own church. Thus she listened both in Washington and in Boston, her home city, to men who were patriots as well as priests.

As she tells the story, one sees how almost all the circumstances of her environment tended to promote her love of country and to stir the emotions of her deeply religious nature. It was by no accident that the national song which bears her name is a hymn. Written at that time and amid those surroundings, it could not have been anything else.

Among her cherished memories of this visit was an interview with Abraham Lincoln, arranged for the party by Governor Andrew. "I remember well the sad expression of Mr. Lincoln's deep blue eyes, the only feature of his face which could be called other than plain.... The President was laboring at this time under a terrible pressure of doubt and anxiety."[21]

The culminating event of her stay in Washington was the visit to the Army of the Potomac on the occasion of a review of troops. As the writing of the "Battle Hymn" was the immediate result of the memorable experiences of that day, I shall defer their consideration till the next chapter.

I have thus sketched briefly the train of events and experiences both before and during the Civil War which led up to the composition of this national hymn. The seed had lain germinating for years—at the last it sprang suddenly into being. My mother's mind often worked in this way. It had a strongly philosophic tendency which made her think long and study deeply. But she possessed, also, the fervor of the poet. Her mental processes were often extremely rapid, especially under the stress of strong emotion. She herself thought the quick action of her mind was due to her red-haired temperament. The two opposing characteristics of her intellect, deliberation and speed, were perhaps the result of the mixed strains of her blood inherited from English and French ancestors.

The student of her life will note a number of sudden inspirations, or visions, as we may call them. Before these we can usually trace a long period of meditation and reflection. Her peace crusade, her conversion to the cause of woman suffrage, her dream of a golden time when men and women should work together for the betterment of the world, were all of this description.

The "Battle Hymn" was the most notable of these inspirations. In her *Recollections of the Anti-Slavery Struggle* she ascribes its composition to two causes—the religion of humanity and the passion of patriotism. The former was a plant of slow growth. In her tribute to Theodore Parker,[22] she tells us how this developed under his preaching, and how he prepared his hearers for the war of blood and iron that soon followed.

My mother had long cherished love for her country, but it burned more intensely when the war came, bursting into sudden flame after that memorable day with the soldiers.

"When the war broke out, the passion of patriotism lent its color to the religion of humanity in my own mind, as in many others, and a moment came in which I could say:

Mine eyes have seen the glory of the coming of the Lord!

—and the echo which my words awoke in many hearts made me sure that many other people had seen it also."[23]

IV
"THE BATTLE HYMN OF THE REPUBLIC"

"The crimson flower of battle blooms" in a single night—The vision in the gray morning twilight—It is written down in the half-darkness on her husband's official paper of the U. S. Sanitary Commission—How it was published in the *Atlantic Monthly* and the price paid for it—The John Brown air derived from a camp-meeting hymn—The simple story in her own words.

OVER and over again, so many times that she lost count of them, was my mother asked to describe the circumstances under which she composed "The Battle Hymn of the Republic." Fortunately she wrote them down, so that we are able to give "the simple story" in her own words.

The following account is taken in part from her *Reminiscences* and in part from the leaflet printed in honor of her seventieth birthday, May 27, 1889, by the New England Woman's Club. She was president of this association for about forty years:

"I distinctly remember that a feeling of discouragement came over me as I drew near the city of Washington. I thought of the women of my acquaintance whose sons or husbands were fighting our great battle; the women themselves serving in the hospitals or busying themselves with the work of the Sanitary Commission. My husband, as already said, was beyond the age of military service, my eldest son but a stripling; my youngest was a child of not more than two years. I could not leave my nursery to follow the march of our armies, neither had I the practical deftness which the preparing and packing of sanitary stores demanded. Something seemed to say to me, 'You would be glad to serve, but you cannot help any one; you have nothing to give, and there is nothing for you to do.' Yet, because of my sincere desire, a word was given me to say which did strengthen the hearts of those who fought in the field and of those who languished in prison.

"In the late autumn of the year 1861 I visited the national capital with my husband, Dr. Howe, and a party of friends, among whom were Governor and Mrs. Andrew, Mr. and Mrs. E. P. Whipple, and my dear pastor, Rev. James Freeman Clarke.

"The journey was one of vivid, even romantic, interest. We were about to see the grim Demon of War face to face, and long before we reached the city his presence made itself felt in the blaze of fires along the road, where sat or stood our pickets, guarding the road on which we traveled.

"One day we drove out to attend a review of troops, appointed to take place at some distance from the city. In the carriage with me were James Freeman Clarke and Mr. and Mrs. Whipple. The day was fine, and everything promised well, but a sudden surprise on the part of the enemy interrupted the proceedings before they were well begun. A small body of our men had been surrounded and cut off from their companions, re-enforcements were sent to their assistance, and the expected pageant was necessarily given up. The troops who were to have taken part in it were ordered back to their quarters, and we also turned our horses' heads homeward.

"For a long distance the foot soldiers nearly filled the road. They were before and behind, and we were obliged to drive very slowly. We presently began to sing some of the well-known songs of the war, and among them:

'John Brown's body lies a-moldering in the grave.'

This seemed to please the soldiers, who cried, 'Good for you,' and themselves took up the strain. Mr. Clarke said to me, 'You ought to write some new words to that tune.' I replied that I had often wished to do so.

"In spite of the excitement of the day I went to bed and slept as usual, but awoke next morning in the gray of the early dawn, and to my astonishment found that the wished-for lines were arranging themselves in my brain. I lay quite still until the last verse had completed itself in my thoughts, then hastily arose, saying to myself, 'I shall lose this if I don't write it down immediately.' I searched for a sheet of paper and an old stump of a pen which I had had the night before and began to scrawl the lines almost without looking, as I had learned to do by often scratching down verses in the darkened room where my little children were sleeping. Having completed this, I lay down again and fell asleep, but not without feeling that something of importance had happened to me."

It will be noted that the first draft of the "Battle Hymn" was written on the back of a sheet of the letter-paper of the Sanitary Commission on which her husband was then serving. Mr. A. J. Bloor, the assistant secretary of that body, has called attention to this. His account of the eventful day is given at the close of this chapter.

My mother gave the original draft of the "Battle Hymn" to her friend, Mrs. Edwin P. Whipple, "who begged it of me, years ago." Hence below the letter-heading:

SANITARY COMMISSION, WASHINGTON, D. C.
TREASURY BUILDING
1861

we find the inscription

WILLARD'S HOTEL
JULIA W. HOWE
TO
CHARLOTTE B. WHIPPLE

The draft remained for many years in the possession of the latter, until it was sent to Messrs. Houghton & Mifflin, in order to have a facsimile made for the *Reminiscences*.

Mr. and Mrs. Whipple were among the familiar friends of our household in those days. The former achieved brilliant successes both as a writer and as a lecturer. He was greatly interested in the anti-slavery agitation; "His eloquent voice was raised more than once in the cause of human freedom." The younger members of our family remember him best for his ready and delightful wit. The fact that he was decidedly homely seemed to give additional point to his funny sayings. Mrs. Whipple was as handsome as her husband was plain—sweet-tempered and sympathetic, yet not wanting in firmness.

Before publishing the poem the author made a number of changes, all of which are, as I think, improvements. The last verse, which is an anticlimax, was cut out altogether.

We find from her letters that she hesitated to allow the publication of the original draft of the "Battle Hymn"[24] because it contained this final verse. She did not consider it equal to the rest of the poem.[25] After consulting other literary people, in her usual painstaking way, she decided to have the first draft published.[26] It will be noted that in the first verse "vintage" has been substituted for "wine press." The first line of the third verse read originally,

> I have read a burning gospel writ in fiery rows of steel.

The later version,

> I have read a fiery gospel, writ in burnished rows of steel:

brings out more clearly the image of the long lines of bayonets as they glittered in her sight on that autumn afternoon. In the fourth verse the second line was somewhat vague in the first draft,

> He has waked the earth's dull bosom with a high ecstatic beat,

The allusion was probably to the marching feet of the armed multitude. The new version,

> He is sifting out the hearts of men before his judgment-seat:

is more direct and simple, hence accords better with the deeply religious tone of the poem.

In the last stanza,

> In the whiteness of the lilies he was born across the sea,

now reads,

> In the beauty of the lilies Christ was born across the sea,

A number of people have asked the meaning of this line. The allusion is evidently to the lilies carried by the angel, in pictures of the annunciation to the Virgin, these flowers being the emblem of purity.

The original version of the second line read,

> With a glory in his bosom that shines out on you and me,

The present words,

> Transfigures you and me,

give us a clearer and more beautiful image. The passion of the poem seems, indeed, to lift on high and glorify our poor humanity.

It is interesting to note that my mother associated with her husband the line,

> *He has sounded forth the trumpet that shall never call retreat,*

Not long before her death, new buildings were erected at Watertown, Massachusetts, for the Perkins Institution for the Blind, founded and administered for more than forty years by Dr. Howe. His son-in-law, Michael Anagnos, ably continued the work during thirty more years.

When we were talking about a suitable inscription in memory of the latter, I suggested to my mother the use of this line. The answer was, "*No, that is for your father.*"

The original draft of the "Battle Hymn" is dated November, 1861; it was published in the *Atlantic Monthly* for February, 1862. The verses were printed on the first page, being thus given the place of honor. According to the custom of that day, no name was signed to them. James T. Fields was then editor of the magazine. My mother consulted him with regard to a name for the poem. It was he, as I think, who christened it "The Battle Hymn of the Republic." The price paid for it was five dollars. But the true price of it was a very different thing, not to be computed in terms of money. It brought its author name and fame throughout the civilized world, in addition to the love and honor of her countrymen. As she grew older and the spiritual beauty of her life and thought shone out more and more clearly, the affection in which she was held deepened into something akin to veneration.

The "Battle Hymn" soon found its way from the pages of the *Atlantic Monthly* into the newspapers, thence to army hymn-books and broadsides. It has been printed over and over again, in a great variety of forms, sometimes with the picture of the author, as in the Perry prints. A white silk handkerchief now in my possession bears the line,

> Mine eyes have seen the glory of the coming of the Lord

worked in red embroidery silk.

My mother was called upon to copy the poem times without number. While she was very willing to write a line or even, upon occasion, a verse or two, she objected very decidedly, especially in her later years, to copying the whole poem. Always responsive to the requests of the autograph fiend, she felt that so much should not be asked of her. For it naturally took time and trouble to make the fair copy that came up to her standard. It was with some difficulty that I persuaded her to send a promised copy to Edmund Clarence Stedman, for his collection.

"But mamma, you *said* you would write it out for him."

With a roguish twinkle, she replied, "Yes, but I did not say *when*."

However, the verses were duly executed and sent to the banker-poet.

"The Battle Hymn of the Republic" has been translated into Spanish, Italian, Armenian, and doubtless other languages. New tunes have been composed for it, but they have failed of acceptance. My mother dearly loved music and was a trained musician, hence her choice of a tune was no haphazard selection. She wrote her poem to the "John Brown" air and they cannot be divorced.

I have been so fortunate as to secure from Franklin B. Sanborn an account of the origin of the words and music of the "John Brown" song. Mr. Sanborn, biographer of Thoreau, John Brown, and others, is the last survivor of the brilliant group of writers belonging to the golden age of New England literature.

CONCORD, MASS., *1916*.

DEAR MRS. HALL—I investigated quite thoroughly the air to which the original John Brown folk song was set;...

I happened to be in Boston the day that Fletcher Webster's regiment (the 12th Mass. Volunteers) came up from Fort Warren, landed on Long Wharf, and marched up State Street past the old State House, on their way to take the train for the Front, in the summer of 1861. As they came along, a quartette, of which Capt. Howard Jenkins, then a sergeant in this regiment, was a tenor voice, was singing something sonorous, which I had never heard. I asked my college friend Jacobsen, of Baltimore, who stood near me, "What are they singing?" He replied, "That boy on the sidewalk is selling copies." I approached him and bought a handbill which, without the music, contained the rude words of the John Brown song, which I then heard for the first time, but listened to a thousand times afterward during the progress of the emancipating Civil War—before they were superseded by Mrs. Howe's inspired lines, which now take their place almost everywhere.

The chorus was borne by the marching soldiers, who had practised it in their drills at the Fort; indeed, it had been adapted from a camp-meeting hymn to a marching song, for which it is admirably fitted, by the bandmaster of Col. Webster's regiment, and afterward revised by Dodworth's military band, then the best in the country. It was this thrilling music, with its resounding religious chorus, which Mrs. Howe, in company with our Massachusetts Governor Andrew, heard near the Potomac, the next November, in the evening camps that encircled Washington.

Yours ever,

F. B. SANBORN.

The following account of Mrs. Howe's visit to Washington and of the circumstances connected with the writing of the "Battle Hymn" was written by Mr. A. J. Bloor, assistant secretary of the U. S. Sanitary Commission:

"JULIA WARD HOWE

"It was the writer's privilege to be introduced early in the Civil War to Julia Ward Howe, the author of 'The Battle Hymn of the Republic,' and now, through the fullness of her days, the dean of American literature, though recognized long ago as having employed her high gift of utterance not merely as the magnet to attract to herself an advantageous celebrity, but paramountly as the instrument for the righting of wrong and the amelioration of the current conditions of humanity."I was presented to Mrs. Howe by her husband, Dr. Samuel Gridley Howe, a companion of Lord Byron in aiding the Greeks to throw off the yoke of the Turks, and the philanthropist who opened the gates of hope to the famous Laura Bridgman, born blind, deaf, and dumb. Dr. Howe invented various processes by which he rescued her from her living tomb, as he subsequently did others born to similar deprivations, and he was careful to leave on record such exhaustive and clear statements as to his methods that, after his decease, the track was well illumined wherein later any well-doer for other victims in like case might open to them, through their single physical sense of touch, the doors leading to all earthly knowledge so far stored in letters...."Dr. Howe, on the outbreak of the Civil War, consented to serve as a member of the U. S. Sanitary Commission, a volunteer organization of influential Union men, springing from a central association in New York City for the relief of the forces serving in the war, and consisting of a few Union ladies, one of whom, Miss Louisa Lee Schuyler, suggested the formation of a similar but larger and wider-spread body of men, representing the Union sentiment of the whole North, into which her own society should be merged as one of—so it turned out—many branches."Such a body was accordingly enrolled and, with Dr. Bellows, a prominent Unitarian clergyman of the day, as its president, was appointed a commission, by President Lincoln, as a *quasi* Bureau of the War Department, to complement the appliances and work of the Government's Medical Bureau and Commissariat, which, at the sudden outbreak of the war, were very deficient."Of this commission I was the assistant secretary, with headquarters at its central office in Washington.... On the occasion of General McClellan's first great review of the Army of the Potomac—numbering at that time about seventy thousand men—at Upton's Hill, in Virginia, not far from the enemy's lines, Dr. Howe asked me to accompany him thither on horseback to see it, which I did. Mrs. Howe had preceded us, with several friends, by carriage, and it was there, in the midst of the blare and glitter and bedizened simulacra of actual and abhorrent warfare, that he did me the honor of presenting me to his wife, then known, outside her private circle, only as the author of a book of charming lyrical essays; but for years since recognized, and doubtless, in the future, will be adjudged, the inspired creator of a war song which for rapt outlook, reverent mysticism, and stateliness of expression, as well as for more widely appreciated patriotic ardor, has more claim, in my estimation, to be styled a hymn than not a few that swell the pages of some of our hymnals. I have always thought it an honor even for the Sanitary Commission with all its noble work of help to the nation in its straits, and of mercy to the suffering, that Julia Ward Howe's 'Battle Hymn of the Republic' should have been written on paper headed 'U. S. Sanitary Commission,' as may be seen by a facsimile of it in her delightful volume of reminiscences. It seems a pity that Mrs. Howe, an accomplished musical composer in private, as well as a poet in public, should not herself have set the air for her own words in that famous utterance of insight, enthusiasm, and prophecy."

V
THE ARMY TAKES IT UP

Gloom in Libby Prison, July 6, 1863—The victory of Gettysburg—Chaplain McCabe sings "Mine eyes have seen the glory of the coming of the Lord"—Five hundred voices take up the chorus—The "Battle Hymn" at the national capital—The great throng shout, sing, and weep—Abraham Lincoln listens with a strange glory on his face—The army takes up the song.

"THE Battle Hymn of the Republic" was inspired by the tremendous issues of the war, as they were brought vividly to the poet's mind by the sight of the Union Army.

My mother had seen all that she describes—she had been a part of the great procession of "burnished rows of steel" when her carriage was surrounded by the Army. She had heard the soldiers singing:

"John Brown's body lies a-moldering in the grave,

His soul is marching on."

Old John Brown who had

>Died to make men free,

whose spirit the army knew to be with them!

All this sank deeply into the heart of the poet. The soul of the Army took possession of her. The song which she wrote down in the gray twilight of that autumn morning voiced the highest aspirations of the soldiers, of the whole people. Hence, when the armies of freedom heard it, they at once hailed it as their own. My mother writes in her *Reminiscences*:

"The poem, which was soon after published in the *Atlantic Monthly*, was somewhat praised on its appearance, but the vicissitudes of the war so engrossed public attention that small heed was taken of literary matters. I knew, and was content to know, that the poem soon found its way to the camps, as I heard from time to time of its being sung in chorus by the soldiers."

This was the beginning, but the interest increased as the "Battle Hymn" became more and more widely known, until it grew to be one of the leading lyrics of the war. It was "sung, chanted, recited, and used in exhortation and prayer on the eve of battle." "It was the word of the hour, and the Union armies marched to its swing."

The "singing chaplain"—Rev. Charles Cardwell McCabe of the 122d Ohio Regiment of Volunteers, did much to popularize this war lyric. Reading it in the *Atlantic Monthly*, he was so charmed with the lines that he committed them to memory before arising from his chair. A year or so later, while attending the wounded men of his regiment, after the battle of Winchester (June, 1863), he was taken prisoner and carried to Libby Prison. Here he was a living benediction to the prisoners. Deeply religious by nature and blest with a cheerful, happy disposition, he kept up the spirits of his companions, ministering alike to their bodily and spiritual needs. Thus he begged three bath-tubs for them, an inestimable treasure, even though these had to serve the needs of six hundred men. Books, too, he procured for them, for the prisoners at this time comprised a notable company of men—doctors, teachers, editors, merchants, lawyers. "We bought books when we needed bread," the chaplain tells us.

With the music of his wonderful voice he was wont to dispel the gloom that often settled upon the inmates of the prison. Many stories are told of its power, pathos, and magnetism. Whenever the dwellers in old Libby felt depression settling upon their spirits they would call out, "Chaplain, sing us a song." Then "The heavy load that oppressed us all seemed as by magic to be lifted."

[27]July 6, 1863, was a dark day for the prisoners. They were required to cast lots for the selection of two captains who were to be executed. These officers were taken to the dungeon below and told to prepare for death. Then the remaining men huddled together discussing the situation. The Confederate forces were marching north, and a terrible battle had been fought. Grant was striving to capture Vicksburg, the key to the Mississippi, with what result they did not know. The Richmond newspapers brought tidings of disaster to the Union armies. In startling head-lines the prisoners read: "Meade defeated at Gettysburg." "The Northern Army fleeing to the mountains." "Grant repulsed at Vicksburg." "The campaign closed in disaster."

A pall deeper and darker than death settled upon the Union prisoners. The poor, emaciated fellows broke down and cried like babies. They lost all hope. "We had not enough strength left to curse God and die," as one of them said later.

"By and by 'Old Ben,' a negro servant, slipped in among them under pretense of doing some work about the prison; concealed under his coat was a later edition of the paper, on which the ink was scarcely dry. He looked around upon the prostrate host, and called out, 'Great news in de papers.' If you have never seen a resurrection, you could not tell what happened. We sprang to our feet and snatched the papers from his hands. Some one struck a light and held aloft a dim candle. By its light we read these head-lines:

'Lee is defeated! His pontoons are swept away! The Potomac is over its banks! The whole North is up in arms and sweeping down upon him!'

"The revulsion of feeling was almost too great to endure. The boys went crazy with joy. They saw the beginning of the end." Chaplain McCabe sprang upon a box and began to sing:

"Mine eyes have seen the glory of the coming of the Lord—"

and the five hundred voices sang the chorus, "Glory, Glory, Hallelujah," as men never sang before. The old negro rolled upon the floor in spasms of joy. I must not forget to add that the two captains were *not* executed, after all.

Chaplain McCabe remained in Libby Prison until October, 1863, when an attack of typhoid fever nearly cost him his life. As soon as his health would permit, he resumed his labors in behalf of the Army, this time as a delegate of the United States Christian Commission. His deep religious feeling, of which patriotism was an integral part, had a great influence among the soldiers. Wherever he went he took the "Battle Hymn" with him. "He sang it to the soldiers in camp and field and hospital; he sang it in school-houses and churches; he sang it at camp-meetings, political gatherings, and the Christian Commission assemblies, and all the Northland took it up."[28]

As he wrote the author:

"I have sung it a thousand times since and shall continue to sing it as long as I live. No hymn has ever stirred the nation's heart like 'The Battle Hymn of the Republic.'"

I must not forget to say that the singing chaplain made excellent use of this war lyric to raise funds for the work among the soldiers. With his matchless voice he sang thousands of dollars out of the people's pockets into the treasury of the Christian Commission.

On February 2, 1864, a meeting in the interests of the Christian Commission was held in the hall of the House of Representatives at Washington. Hannibal Hamlin, Vice-President of the United States, presided. Abraham Lincoln was present, and an immense audience filled the hall. Various noted men spoke; then Chaplain McCabe made a short speech and, "by request," sang the "Battle Hymn." The effect on the great throng was magical. "Men and women sprang to their feet and wept and shouted and sang, as the chaplain led them in that glorious 'Battle Hymn';

they saw Abraham Lincoln's tear-stained face light up with a strange glory as he cried out, '*Sing it again!*' and McCabe and all the multitude sang it again."[29]

Doubtless many Grand Army posts have among their records stories of the inspiring influence of this song in times of trouble or danger. Such an anecdote was related at the Western home of Mrs. Caroline M. Severance, where Acker Post had been invited to meet my mother:

"Capt. Isaac Mahan affectingly described a certain march on a winter midnight through eastern Tennessee. The troops had been for days without enough clothing, without enough food. They were cold and wet that stormy night, hungry, weary, discouraged, morose. But some one soldier began, in courageous tones, to sing 'Mine eyes have seen—' Before the phrase was finished a hundred more voices were heard about the hopeful singer. Another hundred more distant and then another followed until, far to the front and away to the rear, above the splashing tramp of the army through the mud, above the rattle of the horsemen, the rumble of the guns, the creaking of the wagons, and the shouts of the drivers, there echoed, louder and softer, as the rain and wind-gusts varied, the cheerful, dauntless invocation of the 'Battle Hymn.' It was heard as if a heavenly ally were descending with a song of succor, and thereafter the wet, aching marchers thought less that night of their wretched selves, thought more of their cause, their families, their country."

Mr. A. J. Bloor, assistant secretary of the United States Sanitary Commission, has given us some vivid pictures of the soldiers as they sang the hymn:

"Time and again, around the camp-fires scattered at night over some open field, when the Army of the Potomac—or a portion of it—was on the march, have I heard the 'Battle Hymn of the Republic'—generally, however, the first verse only, but in endless repetition—sung in unison by hundreds of voices—occasions more impressive than that of any oratorio sung by any musical troupe in some great assembly-room. And I remember how, one night in the small hours, returning to Washington from the front, by Government steamer up the Potomac, with a party of 'San. Com.' colleagues and Army officers, mostly surgeons, we found our horses awaiting us at the Seventh Street dock; and how, mounting them, we galloped all the long distance to our quarters, singing the 'Battle Hymn'—this time the whole of it—at the top of our voices."

VI
NOTABLE OCCASIONS WHERE IT HAS BEEN SUNG

By great crowds in the street after Union victories in the Civil War—On the downfall of Boss Croker—At Memorial Day celebrations from the Atlantic to the Pacific—At the Chicago convention where the General Federation of Women's Clubs indorsed woman suffrage—At Brown University and Smith College when Mrs. Howe received the degree of LL.D.

"THE Battle Hymn of the Republic" has been sung and recited thousands of times, by all sorts of people under widely varying circumstances, yet the key-note of it is most fitly struck when men and women are lifted out of themselves by the power of strong emotion. In times of danger and of thanksgiving the "Battle Hymn" is now, as it was in the 'sixties, the fitting vehicle for the expression of national feeling. Indeed, it has been so used in other countries as well as in our own. In my mother's journal the entry often occurs, "They sang my 'Battle Hymn.'" Usually she makes no comment.

It would, of course, be impossible and it might be tedious to rehearse all the notable occasions where this national song has been given. Yet many of them have been so full of interest as to demand a place in the story of the "Battle Hymn." The record would be incomplete without them. I give a few which will serve as samples.

In New York City there was a good deal of disloyal sentiment during the Civil War. Here the draft riots took place in the summer of 1863, when the guns from the battle of Gettysburg were rushed to the metropolis. Here the cannon, their wheels still deeply incrusted with mud, were drawn up, a grim reminder to the rioters of the actual meaning of war. To these the sight of a uniform was odious. My husband, David Prescott Hall, then a young lad returning from a summer camping trip, was chased through the streets by some excited individuals. As he had a knapsack on his back, they mistook him for a soldier.

It need scarcely be said that New York City had also a large loyal population. In the early days of the war men suspected of secession sympathies were visited by deputations of citizens who insisted upon their displaying the flag. They found it wiser to do so. After one of the final victories of the war, perhaps the taking of Richmond, a great crowd gathered before the bulletin-board of a New York newspaper. Some one started to sing the "Battle Hymn" and the whole mass of people took it up, "*Glory, Glory, Hallelujah!*" What else could so well have expressed the joy and thanksgiving of our people, weary of four long years of fratricidal war! My husband, who was present, described the scene as being most impressive.

F. B. Sanborn in his *Early History of Kansas* tells us an interesting story of the singing of the "Battle Hymn" on a very different occasion.

"People were gathered together to hear a sermon from Col. James Montgomery, a man of undaunted courage and a veteran both of the Civil War and of the Kansas struggle. The place was Trading Post, where, during the Kansas troubles, some fourteen years before this time, a massacre had been perpetrated. Among his audience were survivors and relatives of the slain. There were present, too, a score of men who had 'shouted amen when their renowned leader registered his vow that the blood of the dead and the tears of the widows and children should not be shed in vain.' Montgomery was of the indomitable Scotch-Irish blood, tall and slender, with a shaggy shock of long black hair and even shaggier whiskers.

"As he arose to begin the services and fixed his gaze on the familiar faces of those who had suffered and whose sufferings he had so fully avenged, a gleam of joy and satisfaction seemed to blaze from his penetrating eyes and thrilled the audience into perfect accord. He hesitated a moment, and then requested all to arise and sing 'The Battle Hymn of the Republic.' The noble thought of that grand hymn stirred the crowd to the deepest depths of feeling. The text was in keeping with the occasion:

"'Be not deceived. God is not mocked, for whatsoever a man soweth, that shall he also reap.'

"The discourse was powerful and impressive. He reminded his hearers of his prophecy that the remaining years of slavery could be numbered on the fingers of one hand, and that he should lead a host of negro soldiers, arrayed in the national uniform, in the redemption of the country from the curse of slavery. A few days afterward the old Covenanter was dead!"

To the Grand Army of the Republic Julia Ward Howe was especially dear. On Memorial Day a detachment always visits and decorates her grave, with simple but impressive ceremonies. Upon that of her husband, which lies next to hers, the Greeks always lay flowers. This festival of remembrance comes only three days after my mother's birthday, May 27th. In 1899, when she was eighty years of age, the ceremonies in Boston were of unusual interest.

The Grand Army of the Republic held a celebration in Boston Theater, Major-General Joseph Wheeler, formerly an officer in the Confederate Army, having been invited to deliver the address. Mrs. Howe rode thither in an open carriage with the general's two daughters, "*very* pleasant girls."

The Philadelphia *Press* thus describes the occasion:

"BOSTON WARMED UP

"The major has just returned from Boston, where he was present at the Memorial Day services held in Boston Theater.

"It was the real thing. I never imagined possible such a genuine sweeping emotion as when that audience began to sing the 'Battle Hymn.' If Boston was cold, it was thawed by the demonstration on Tuesday. Myron W. Whitney started to sing. He bowed to a box, in which we first recognized Mrs. Howe, sitting with the Misses Wheeler. You should have heard the yell. We could see the splendid white head trembling; then her voice joined in, as Whitney sang, 'In the beauty of the lilies,' and by the time he had reached the words, 'As He died to make men holy, let us die to make men free,' the whole vast audience was on its feet, sobbing and singing at the top of its thousands of lungs. If volunteers were really needed for the Philippines, McKinley could have had us all right there."

This was in her adopted city of Boston, where she had lived for more than half a century. The Grand Army men of California gave her a similar reception on Memorial Day, 1888.

We quote extracts from the San Francisco papers describing it:

"The Grand Opera House never contained a larger audience. Not only were all the chairs taken up but every inch of standing-room was pre-empted. There were many persons who could not gain an entrance.... Mr. Dibble next called the attention of the audience to the fact that Mrs. Julia Ward Howe, the author of 'The Battle Hymn of the Republic,' was among the guests of the evening.

"At this juncture an enthusiastic gentleman in one of the front seats sprang up and called for three cheers for Mrs. Howe. They were given with a vim, Mrs. Howe acknowledging the compliment by rising and bowing.... The next event upon the program was the singing of 'The Battle Hymn of the Republic' by J. C. Hughes. The singing was preceded by a scene rarely witnessed and which was not on the printed program. General Salomon introduced Mrs. Howe to the audience in an appreciative speech.

"A beautiful floral piece was then presented to Mrs. Howe, which she acknowledged in fitting terms, while the audience gave three cheers and a tiger for the author of 'The Battle Hymn of the Republic.'

"Mrs. Howe advanced to the footlights, beaming with pleasure. She then said:

"'My dear friends, I cannot, with my weak voice, reach this vast assemblage; but I will endeavor to have some of you hear me. I join in this celebration with thrilled and uplifted heart. I remember those camp-fires, I remember those dreadful battles. It was a question with us women, "Will our men prevail? Until they do, they will not come home." How we blessed them when they did; how we blessed them with our prayers when they were on the battle-field. Those were times of sorrow; this is one of joy. Let us thank God who has given us these victories.'

"As Mrs. Howe was about to resume her seat the audience rose *en masse*, and from the dress-circle to the upper gallery rung a round of cheers.

"The audience remained standing while Mr. Hughes sang the stirring words of the hymn, and joined heartily in the chorus as by request. At the last chorus Mrs. Howe stepped forward and joined in the song, closing with a general flutter of handkerchiefs."

My mother visited the Pacific coast twice in the latter years of her life, as her beloved sister, Mrs. Adolphe Mailliard, then lived there. She was received in a way that was very gratifying to her and her family.

One of the most dearly prized privileges of a self-governing people is that of constant grumbling over the administration of affairs and of finding fault with our rulers—who, in the last analysis, are ourselves. In England men write to the *Times*; in America we write to many papers and we complain endlessly. This would evidently be impossible under a despotic Government, and it sometimes seems as if we indulged too freely in depreciating our own country and its institutions. Yet deep down in the hearts of our people is a love of our native land which flames forth brightly on great occasions. The country which produced the "Battle Hymn" is not lacking in true patriotism. So long as our people use it to express their deepest emotions we need fear no serious treason to the Republic. The danger of our frequent fault-finding is that we thus allow our righteous indignation to evaporate in mere words.

Supineness in politics, an indolence which permits unworthy men to usurp the reins of government, is one of our great sins as a nation. Yet the corrupt manipulator who goes too far meets an uprising of popular indignation which thoroughly surprises him. From the New York *Sun* we quote the story of such a day of retribution.

At the downfall of Boss Croker "a throng gathered in Madison Square. Not even in a Presidential election in recent years have there been such innumerable hosts as gathered in front of the Fifth Avenue Hotel and the

Hoffman House last night to hear of the doom of Croker and his cronies. Cheer upon cheer ascended when the mighty army read that Low was far ahead and would win in the great battle." Some one struck up the "Battle Hymn." "All over the square were heard the thousands singing this great hymn.... There has not been such a scene in New York City since war days."

Among the notable occasions we must certainly count the unveiling of the Shaw Monument. Here the art of St.-Gaudens has preserved in immemorial stone the story of Robert Gould Shaw and his colored soldiers, the heroes of Fort Wagner. The monument stands just within old Boston Common, facing the State House. The ceremonies of dedication included a procession and a meeting in Music Hall, where Prof. William James and Booker Washington made the principal addresses, and the "Battle Hymn" was sung.

My mother is best known as the author of the "Battle Hymn." Soon after the war she began her efforts in behalf of the woman's cause, which eventually won for her the great affection of her countrywomen as well as a reputation extending to foreign shores. She was deeply interested both in the club and in the suffrage movement. She lived to see the full flowering of the former and the partial success of the latter. Despite the many weary trials and delays she never lost faith in the ultimate victory of the suffrage cause. "I shall live to see women win the franchise in New York State," she declared, not many years before her death.

In the early days of the club movement my mother, like most of her fellow-suffragists, thought it best not to mingle the two issues. While the more advanced thinkers among the club women believed in the enfranchisement of their sex, the majority did not.

At last the two movements—like two rapidly flowing streams that have long been drawing nearer together—joined in one mighty river. I have often wished my mother could have lived to see that wonderful day at Chicago when the General Federation of Women's Clubs—an association comprising more than one and a half million women—declared themselves, amid cheers and tears, in favor of votes for women. Every one was deeply moved; the delegates embraced one another, and the "Battle Hymn" was sung—a hymn this time of joyous thanksgiving for the victory obtained, yet of solemn dedication, too, to the hard labor still to be performed before the good fight could be fully won.

My mother describes one occasion where the "Battle Hymn" was given in dumb show before the Association for the Advancement of Women. She was very much attached to this pioneer society, of which she was the president during many years. The association held annual congresses in different parts of the United States, the proceedings eliciting much interest. When they were at X—— one of the members invited the society to visit a school for young girls of which she was the principal.

"After witnessing some interesting exercises we assemble in the large hall, where a novel entertainment has been provided for us. A band of twelve young ladies appear upon the platform. They wear the colors of 'Old Glory,' but after a new fashion, four of them being arrayed from head to foot in red, four in blue, and four in white. While the 'John Brown' tune is heard from the piano, they proceed to act in graceful dumb show the stanzas of my 'Battle Hymn.' How they did it I cannot tell, but it was a most lovely performance."[30]

In the early days of the woman movement a hard struggle was necessary in order to secure for girls the advantages of the higher education. Into this my mother threw herself with her accustomed zeal. A lifelong student and lover of books, she ardently desired to secure for other women the advantages she herself so highly prized. Enjoying robust health, and accustomed to prolonged mental labor, she never doubted the capacity of her sex for serious study. So, despite the gloomy prognostications of learned doctors (all men), she and her fellow-suffragists persevered until the battle was won. Thus it was very fitting that the three institutions which bestowed honorary degrees upon her—Tufts College, Brown University, and Smith College—all counted women among their students. Her youngest daughter, Maud Howe Elliott, thus describes the scene at Providence:[31]

"On June 16th (1909) Brown University, her husband's *alma mater* and her grandfather's, conferred upon her the degree of Doctor of Laws.... Her name was called last. With the deliberate step of age, she walked forward, wearing her son's college gown over her white dress, his mortar-board cap over her lace veil. She seemed less moved than any person present; she could not see what we saw, the tiny gallant figure bent with four score and ten years of study and hard labor. As she moved between the girl students who stood up to let her pass, she whispered: 'How tall they are! It seems to me the girls are much taller than they used to be.' Did she realize how much shorter she was than she once had been? I think not. Then, her eyes sparkling with fun while all other eyes were wet, she shook her hard-earned diploma with a gay gesture in the faces of those girls, cast on them a keen glance that somehow was a challenge, 'Catch up with me if you can!'" The band played the air of the "Battle Hymn" and applause followed her as she went back to her seat.

"She had labored long for the higher education of women, suffered estrangement, borne ridicule for it—the sight of those girl graduates, starting on their life voyage equipped with a good education, was like a sudden realization of a lifelong dream, uplifted her, gave her strength for the fatigues of the day."

A similar scene was enacted in October, 1910, shortly before her death, when Smith College conferred the same degree upon her.

"Opposite the platform, as if hung in air, a curving gallery was filled with white-clad girls, some two thousand of them; as she entered they rose like a flock of doves, and with them the whole audience. They rose once more when her name was called, last in the list of those honored with degrees, and as she came forward, the organ pealed, and the great chorus of fresh young voices broke out with—

"'Mine eyes have seen the glory of the coming of the Lord,'

"It was the last time."[32]

VII
HOW AND WHERE THE AUTHOR RECITED IT

> The simplicity and deep earnestness of her manner—Her clear and musical voice which never grew old—How Susan B. Anthony "mixed up" two songs—Gladdened by the love and honor which it brought her, Mrs. Howe repeats the "Battle Hymn" in all parts of the country before all sorts of audiences, small and great—Why its appeal to the human heart is universal.

IT may be imagined that the heart of the woman who wrote the "Battle Hymn" was greatly gladdened by the love and honor which it brought her. She enjoyed to the full the beautiful affection shown her by her countrymen and countrywomen, and, in my opinion, her happy and sympathetic relations with them prolonged her life. She was glad to live, despite the physical weakness of old age, because she knew that she was widely beloved and could still be of use. Her mind remained clear and brilliant to the very last.

The honors paid her she received with the humility that dreads over-praise. In her journal she questions her worthiness to be made so much of, and hopes to the end that she may be able to do something of value to mankind.

The recital of her "Battle Hymn" gave so much pleasure that she was very willing to repeat it, under suitable circumstances. She was asked to do so at all times and seasons and in all sorts of places. People who requested her to recite her war lyric at the close of a lecture did not realize the fatigue that it entailed upon a person no longer young and already weary with speaking. Yet I doubt if she ever refused, when it was possible for her to comply with the request. Not long before her death, some ladies, calling upon her at her summer home near Newport, begged her to recite then and there the "Battle Hymn." She was loth to do so, feeling the solemn words were not at all in keeping with the light and pleasant chat of a morning visit. As one of the callers was frankly an old lady, my mother at length consented. According to her custom when asked to recite under such circumstances, she withdrew for a few minutes before beginning.

There are thousands of people now living, I suppose, who have heard the author's recitation of the "Battle Hymn." Yet because there are thousands who never did hear it, and because these things slip so easily out of mind, it is well to give some description of it *"Lest we forget."*

My mother repeated the verses of the hymn simply, yet with a solemnity that was all the more impressive because there was no effort at elocutionary or dramatic effect. Yet there was sufficient variety in the recitation to avoid any approach to monotony. Thus she repeated the lines

"O be swift, my soul, to answer Him, be jubilant, my feet!"

with uplifted hands, a downward glance at her feet, and voice slightly raised. Her distinct enunciation and the clear, musical tones of a voice that never grew old, made the words audible even in a large auditorium.

Her deeply serious manner, corresponding so well as it did with the solemn, prophetic words of the "Battle Hymn," made the recitation very impressive.

We saw before us the woman who had been privileged to speak the word for the hour, in the dark days of her country's history. It was like seeing some priestess of old delivering the sacred oracle to her people. Though the message was repeated so many times, it never lost its power to stir the souls of those who heard it.

It should be said that the habit of speaking very carefully, my mother formed early in life. Having a brother who stammered, she was very anxious to avoid that defect of speech. The beauty of her voice was due to its careful training in the Italian school of singing in her youth. Doubtless the habit of public speaking also tended to preserve it.

She occasionally repeated "The Flag," a more dramatic and more personal poem than the "Battle Hymn." Her rendering of it, accordingly, was more dramatic.

On public occasions my mother was often introduced as "The author of 'The Battle Hymn of the Republic.'" Sometimes the introducer would, by mistake, substitute the name of another war song, good of its kind, but hardly to be compared with my mother's hymn. She used to say, rather plaintively, that Miss Susan B. Anthony (the well-known suffrage leader) *would* mix up the two songs, introducing her as *"The author of the 'Battle Cry of Freedom.'"*

It was a joy to her to be associated with the "Battle Hymn," yet she sometimes grieved a little because this so greatly overshadowed all her other literary productions. She had labored long and earnestly with pen and voice, writing both prose and poetry which won commendation from her comrades in the world of letters. Hence she was glad to be remembered as the author, not only of her war lyric, but of other compositions as well.

My mother was asked to repeat this more and more often as its fame increased and as she herself became ever dearer to her countrymen. As early as 1865 we find that she was urged to recite it at Newport at the close of her lecture in Mr. Richard Hunt's studio. Among those in the audience was George Bancroft, the historian, a prominent figure in Newport society of the olden days. Mr. Bancroft had held various offices under the Federal Government, that of Secretary of the Navy among others. When the Civil War broke out there was a good deal of secession feeling among the summer residents of the watering-place, but Mr. and Mrs. Bancroft were steadfastly loyal to the Union.

It is interesting to note that among the many places where its author recited the "Battle Hymn," at least one city in the heart of the South is included. Mrs. Howe spent the winter of 1884-85 in New Orleans, having been invited to preside over the woman's department of the exposition held there in that year.

The experience involved much hard work, but also much pleasure. She made many friends in the Crescent City, whither she and I returned eleven years later for a congress of the Association for the Advancement of Women. We were the guests of her old friend, Mrs. King, the mother of Grace King, the novelist, and were entertained by mother and daughters with charming hospitality.

I confess that it surprised me when, at an afternoon reception in the King drawing-room, my mother was asked to repeat the "Battle Hymn," and did so. This showed us how much the old ill-feeling between North and South had died out. It demonstrated also the universal and therefore non-sectional quality of the poem, of which more will be said in the following chapter.

The "Battle Hymn" may be called universal in still another sense, since it appeals to men and women of all religious creeds. When Mrs. Howe was especially requested to recite it before a council of Jewish women, it gave her "an unexpected thrill of satisfaction." She was warmly received and welcomed, but felt some anxiety lest the verse beginning "In the beauty of the lilies Christ was born across the sea" might disturb her hearers. The president assured her, however, that there was nothing in it to hurt their feelings.

My mother was so intimately associated with the woman movement that she was called upon to repeat her war lyric before many feminine audiences. We have spoken of her interest in women's clubs. She was also interested in the patriotic societies, being a member of the D. A. R. and of the Colonial Dames of Rhode Island. One of the Boston chapters of the former is named in honor of the Old South Meeting-house, a venerated landmark of the city. When the congregation left their old place of worship and moved to the Back Bay, it required a tremendous effort on the part of the women of Boston to raise the necessary funds and to save the historic building from destruction. Here, in December, 1906, the Old South Chapter had a meeting where there was "much good speaking." My mother recited her "Battle Hymn" and told them something of her Revolutionary ancestors. She remembered her forebears with affectionate pride as noble men and women whose example she strove to imitate.

A long life brings its penalties as well as its pleasures. Living to the age of nearly ninety-two years, my mother survived all the friends of her youth and most, if not all, of her contemporaries. Hence she was called upon to attend many funerals, considering this a duty, in accordance with old-fashioned ideas. A temporary lameness prevented her attending the obsequies of the poet Longfellow, an early friend of her husband's, whom she also had known well for many years. She was able, however, to testify to her friendship for the gentle poet by giving her services for the Longfellow Memorial held at the Boston Museum. Here she took part in an authors' reading, reciting the "Battle Hymn," as well as some verses composed in honor of the poet.

That she should be invited to do so shows a great change in public opinion since the early years of their acquaintance. In the 'forties and 'fifties it was not thought fitting that a lady should even sign her name to a poem or a novel, much less read it in public. When my mother published some verses in a volume edited by Mr. Longfellow in those early days, they appeared as anonymous. By his advice, her first book of poems, *Passion Flowers*, bore no name upon the title-page.

VIII
TRIBUTES TO "THE BATTLE HYMN"

From Abraham Lincoln, Theodore Roosevelt, Conan Doyle, Ralph Waldo Emerson, William Dean Howells,[33] U. S. Senator George F. Hoar, Thomas Starr King, Ina Coolbrith, and others—The "Battle Hymn" and the "Marseillaise"—What Rudyard Kipling said of it in "The Light that Failed"—English reprints distributed among the soldiers of the present war.

THE appeal of "The Battle Hymn of the Republic" is so wide that it takes in all classes of mankind, all, at least, who love freedom.

Wherever rise the peoples,

Wherever sinks a throne,

The throbbing heart of freedom

Finds an answer in his own.

So wrote the poet Whittier of Samuel Gridley Howe, remembering his services to the Greeks, to the Poles and others. The lines are equally true of his wife, Julia Ward Howe, and of the spirit animating her war lyric. Although written in the midst of the greatest civil war that was ever fought and won, there is no word of North or South, no appeal to local pride or patriotism, no word of sectional strife or bitterness. The God to whom appeal is made is the God of freedom. The enemy to be overcome, the serpent who is to be crushed beneath the heel of the hero, is slavery.

It is amusing and yet sad to find that some literal souls have fancied that my mother intended to designate the Southerners by "the grapes of wrath." Needless to say that the writer intended no such narrow and prosaic meaning.

The "Battle Hymn" may well be compared to the "Marseillaise." The man is to be pitied who can hear either of them without a thrill of answering emotion. Both have the power to move their hearers profoundly, yet they are as different as the two nationalities which gave them birth. The French national hymn appeals to us by its wonderfully stirring music more than by the words. We can imagine how the latter aroused to a frenzy of feeling the men of the French Revolution, when they rose to throw off the yoke of centuries of oppression and misrule. Feudalism perished in France to the fiery music of the "Marseillaise." Slavery died in America to the old "John Brown" tune, as slow and steadfast in movement as the Northern race who sang it.

In our war lyric we seem to hear an echo of the old cry, "The sword of the Lord and of Gideon." Yet we did not fully recognize its tremendous power until Kipling christened it *"The terrible Battle Hymn of the Republic."*

In the closing scene of *The Light that Failed*[34] we are shown a group of English newspaper correspondents about to start for a war in the Soudan. They are met together for a last evening of song and merrymaking, yet one of their number "by the instinct of association began to hum the terrible Battle Hymn of the Republic. Man after man caught it up—it was a tune they knew well, till the windows shook to the clang, the Nilghai's deep voice leading:

"'Mine eyes have seen the glory of the coming of the Lord.'"

Sir A. Conan Doyle pays a similar tribute to its power in *Through the Magic Door*:

"Take the songs which they sang during the most bloody war which the Anglo-Celtic race has ever waged—the only war in which it could have been said that they were stretched to their uttermost and showed their true form ... all had a playful humor running through them. Only one exception do I know, and that is the most tremendous war song I can recall; even an outsider in time of peace can hardly read it without emotion. I mean, of course, Julia Ward Howe's war song of the Republic, with the choral opening line,

'Mine eyes have seen the glory of the coming of the Lord.'

If that were ever sung upon a battle-field the effect must have been terrific."

During the present war in Europe, an English lady has had a large number of copies of the "Hymn" printed and distributed, through the Young Men's Christian Association, to the soldiers. They contain the following explanation: "This magnificent 'Battle Hymn of the Republic' was written in 1861 by a famous American lady, Mrs. Julia Ward Howe, for the Army of the Northern States of America, which were then engaged in a 'Holy War' to rid the South of slavery and to preserve the Union of the States. It is said to have done more to awaken the spirit of patriotism and to have inspired more deeds of heroism than any other event of the American Civil War."

It is pleasant and heartening to read these tributes of praise from distinguished Englishmen. That our "Battle Hymn of the Republic" should so strongly appeal to them shows us the essential unity of the two great branches of the Anglo-Saxon race, even though oceans roll between Great Britain and America.

The strange glory that came over the face of Abraham Lincoln and the tears he shed on hearing the "Battle Hymn" will always be, for his countrymen, the most precious tribute to its power.

"The chaplain afterward stated that in his conversation with Mr. Lincoln at his reception, the President said to him, 'Take it all in all, the song and the singing, that was the best I ever heard.'"[35]

To the steadfast and courageous soul of another great American, who also has held the high office of President of these United States, Theodore Roosevelt, this war hymn strongly appealed. His book, *Fear God and Take Your Own Part*, is prefaced by "The Battle Hymn of the Republic" and by the following dedication:

> "This book is dedicated to the memory of
> JULIA WARD HOWE

because in the vital matters fundamentally affecting the life of the Republic she was as good a citizen of the Republic as Washington and Lincoln themselves. She was in the highest sense a good wife and a good mother, and therefore she fulfilled the primary law of our being. She brought up with devoted care and wisdom her sons and her daughters. At the same time she fulfilled her full duty to the commonwealth from the public standpoint. She preached righteousness and she practised righteousness. She sought the peace that comes as the handmaiden of well-doing. She preached that stern and lofty courage of soul which shrinks neither from war nor from any other form of suffering and hardship and danger if it is only thereby that justice can be served. She embodied that trait more essential than any other in the make-up of the men and women of this Republic—the valor of righteousness."

In the letter given below, Hon. George F. Hoar, United States Senator from Massachusetts, compares "The Battle Hymn of the Republic" with the "Marseillaise" and with the "British National Anthem."

WORCESTER, MASS., *May 22, 1903*.

I was thinking, just as I got your letter asking me to send a greeting to your meeting and to Mrs. Howe, of the great power, in framing the character of nations, of their National Anthems. Fletcher of Saltoun said, as every child knows, "Let me make the songs of a people, and I care not who make their laws." No single influence has had so much to do with shaping the destiny of a nation, as nothing more surely expresses national character, than what is known as the National Anthem. France adopted for hers the "Marseillaise." Its stirring appeal

> Sons of France, awake to glory!

led the youth of France to march through Europe, subduing kingdoms and overthrowing dynasties, till "forty centuries looked down on them from the pyramids." At last the ambition of France perished and came to grief, as every unholy ambition is destined to perish and come to grief, and her great Emperor died in exile at St. Helena.

Is there anything more cheap and vulgar than the National Anthem of our English brethren, "God Save the King"?

O Lord our God, arise!

Scatter his enemies

And make them fall.

Confound their politics,

Frustrate their knavish tricks;

On him our hopes we fix;

God save us all!

England, I hope, knows better now. But she has acted on that motto for a thousand years.

New England's Anthem,

> The breaking waves dashed high,

one of the noblest poems in all literature, was written by a woman.

We waited eighty years for our American National Anthem. At last God inspired an illustrious and noble woman to utter in undying verse the thought which we hope is forever to animate the soldier of the Republic.

In the beauty of the lilies Christ was born across the sea,

With a glory in His bosom which transfigures you and me;

As He died to make men holy, let us die to make men free,

While God is marching on!

Julia Ward Howe cannot yet vote in America. But her words will be an inspiration to the youth of America on many a hard-fought field for liberty many a century after her successors will vote.

> I am faithfully yours,

GEORGE F. HOAR.

MISS ALICE STONE BLACKWELL.

In the journals of Ralph Waldo Emerson we find this tribute to his friend, Julia Ward Howe:

"I honour the author of the 'Battle Hymn' and of 'The Flag.' She was born in the city of New York. I could well wish she were a native of Massachusetts. We have had no such poetess in New England."

The little bit of State pride voiced in the regret that my mother was not a native of the old Bay State, surprises us in a man of such wide sympathies as Mr. Emerson. In Whittier's early poems also the local feeling is strongly pronounced. We should remember, however, that during the nineteenth century a good deal of sectional feeling still existed in the different States. The twentieth century finds us more closely united as a people than we have ever been before.

Edmund Clarence Stedman happily characterizes the war hymn in the following passage. It occurs in a letter to me, asking that my mother would copy it for him.

"I can well understand what a Frankenstein's monster such a creation grows to be—such a poem as the 'Battle Hymn' when it has become the sacred scroll of millions, each one of whom would fain obtain a copy of it."[36]

Those who have visited the White Mountains will remember that one of the peaks is called "Starr King." It was named for Thomas Starr King, a noted Unitarian preacher in the middle of the nineteenth century. Shortly before the Civil War he accepted a call to San Francisco. In addition to officiating in the church there he soon took upon his shoulders a task that was too heavy for his somewhat frail physique. This was nothing less than persuading the people of California to remain loyal to the Union. There was a good deal of secession sentiment on the Pacific coast in 1861. Starr King and his fellow-Unionists succeeded in their undertaking, but he paid the penalty of overwork with his life. Hence his memory is beloved and revered on the shores of the Pacific as well as on those of the Atlantic. One can imagine what the "Battle Hymn" must have meant to him, weary as he was with his strenuous labors. He pronounced it "a miraculously perfect poem."

Another "Spray of Western Pine" was contributed to the garland of praise by Ina Coolbrith, one of the last survivors of the golden age of California literature.

JULIA WARD HOWE

When with the awful lightning of His glance,

Jehovah, thro' the mighty walls of sea

His people led from their long bondage free,—

A Woman's hand, too light to lift the lance,

Miriam, the Prophetess, with song and dance,

With timbrel, and with harp and psaltery,

Struck the proud notes of triumphs yet to be,

And voiced her Israel's deliverance.

So in our own dear Land, in strife to save

Another race oppressed, when light grew dim,

And the Red Sea of blood loomed fatefully

To overwhelm, the God of freedom gave

Thro' Woman's lips His sacred battle hymn

That rang thro' combat on to victory!

When memorial services were held in honor of my mother, Boston's great Symphony Hall was crowded to its utmost capacity. Many were the beautiful tributes to her given by men and women of national reputation. None, however, equaled in heartfelt eloquence the speech of Lewis, the distinguished negro lawyer. As he poured out the gratitude of his race to the woman who had written "The Battle Hymn of the Republic," I suddenly realized for the first time what the words meant to the colored people.

>As He died to make men holy, let us die to make men free.

"To make us, black men and black women, free!" The appeal was to the white men of our country, bidding them share the freedom they so dearly prized with the despised slave. And this triumphant gospel of liberty with its stirring chorus of "Glory, glory, hallelujah" was sung wherever the Northern army went. It was the first proclamation of emancipation. If it moves us, how must it have affected the people to whom it was a prophecy of the longed-for deliverance from bondage.

IX
MRS. HOWE'S LESSER POEMS OF THE CIVIL WAR

>Her poetic tribute to Frederick Douglass—"Left Behind," "Our Orders," "April 19"—"The Flag" followed the second battle of Bull Run—"The Secesh" in the Newport churches—"The First Martyr," "Our Country," "Harvard Student's Song," "Return"—How "Our Country" lost its musical setting—"The Parricide" written on the day of Lincoln's funeral to express her reverence.

MY mother's natural mode of expressing herself was by poetry rather than by prose. She wrote verses from her earliest years up to the time of her death. It is true that some of her best work took the form of prose in her essays, lectures, and speeches,[37] yet whenever her feelings were deeply moved she turned to verse as the fittest vehicle for her use.

We have seen that she began to write poems protesting against human slavery at an early period of her career. Thus her first published "On the Death of the Slave Lewis." In *Words for the Hour* we find several poems dealing with slavery, the struggle in Kansas, the attack on Sumner, and kindred subjects. The titles of these and some quotations from them are given in Chapter I. The verses on "Tremont Temple" contain tributes to Sumner and Frederick Douglass, the negro orator. The first two are as follows: volume, *Passion Flowers* (1853), contained verses

Two figures fill this temple to my sight,

Whoe'er shall speak, their forms behind him stand;

One has the beauty of our Northern blood,

And wields Jove's thunder in his lifted hand.

The other wears the solemn hue of Night

Drawn darker in the blazonry of pain,

Blotting the gaslight's mimic day, he slings

A dangerous weapon, too, a broken chain.

When the Civil War broke out, she poured forth the feelings that so deeply moved her in a number of poems. "The Battle Hymn of the Republic" is the best known of these, as it deserves to be. The others, however, while varying as to merit, show the same patriotism, indignation against wrong, and elevation of spirit. The woman's tenderness of heart breathes through them, too, as in the story of the dying soldier:

LEFT BEHIND

The foe is retreating, the field is clear;

My thoughts fly like lightning, my steps stay here;

I'm bleeding to faintness, no help is near:

What, ho! comrades; what, ho!

The battle was deadly, the shots fell thick;

We leaped from our trenches, and charged them quick;

I knew not my wound till my heart grew sick:

So there, comrades; so there.

We charged the left column, that broke and fled;

Poured powder for powder, and lead for lead:

So they must surrender, what matter who's dead?

Who cares, comrades? who cares?

My soul rises up on the wings of the slain,

A triumph thrills through me that quiets the pain:

If it were yet to do, I would do it again!

Farewell, comrades, farewell!

It will be remembered that the first blood shed in the Civil War was in Baltimore. There the Massachusetts troops, while on their way to defend the national capital, were attacked by "Plug-Uglies" and several soldiers were killed. My mother thus describes the funeral in Boston:[38]

"We were present when these bodies were received at King's Chapel burial-ground, and could easily see how deeply the Governor was moved at the sad sight of the coffins draped with the national flag. This occasion drew from me the poem:

"OUR ORDERS

"Weave no more silks, ye Lyons Looms;

To deck our girls for gay delights!

The crimson flower of battle blooms,

And solemn marches fill the night.

"Weave but the flag whose bars to-day

Drooped heavy o'er our early dead,

And homely garments, coarse and gray,

For orphans that must earn their bread!"

(We give the first two of the six verses.)

Other verses published in *Later Lyrics* under the title "April 19" commemorate the same event. They were evidently written in the first heat of indignation at the breaking out of the rebellion, yet her righteous wrath always gave way to a second thought, tenderer and more merciful than the first. We see this in the last verse of the "Battle Hymn" and in various other poems of hers. The opening verses of "April 19" are:

A spasm o'er my heart

Sweeps like a burning flood;

A sentence rings upon mine ears,

Avenge the guiltless blood!

Sit not in health and ease,

Nor reckon loss nor gain,

When men who bear our Country's flag

Are set upon and slain.

Of her "Poems of the War" "The Flag" ranks second in popular esteem and has a place in many anthologies. She thus describes the circumstances under which it was composed:[39]

"Even in gay Newport there were sad reverberations of the strife. I shall never forget an afternoon on which I drove into town with my son, by this time a lad of fourteen, and found the main street lined with carriages, and the carriages filled with white-faced people, intent on I knew not what. Meeting a friend, I asked: 'Why are these people here? What are they waiting for and why do they look as they do?'

"'They are waiting for the mail. Don't you know that we have had a dreadful reverse?' Alas! this was the second battle of Bull Run. I have made some record of it in a poem entitled 'The Flag,' which I dare mention here because Mr. Emerson, on hearing it, said to me, 'I like the architecture of that poem.'"

The opening verse is as follows:

There's a flag hangs over my threshold, whose folds are more dear to me

Than the blood that thrills in my bosom its earnest of liberty;

And dear are the stars it harbors in its sunny field of blue

As the hope of a further heaven, that lights all our dim lives through.

Before the war, Newport had been a favorite resort for Southerners. During the summer of 1861 a number were still there, and it must be confessed some of them behaved with very little tact. According to reports current at the time, these individuals carried politics inside the church doors. When the prayer for the President of the United States was read, they arose from their knees in order to show their disapproval. At its conclusion they again knelt. Women would draw aside the voluminous skirts then in fashion, to prevent their coming in contact with the United States flag. I have always fancied that the lines in "The Flag,"

> Salute the flag in its virtue, or pass on where others rule,

were inspired by this behavior of "The Secesh," as we then called them. Some of these persons, although belonging to good society, had the bad taste to boast in our presence of how the South was going to "whip" the North. At a certain picnic among the Paradise Rocks, my mother resolved to give these people a lesson in patriotism. One of our number, a quiet, elderly lady, was selected to act as America, the queen of the occasion. She was crowned with flowers, and we all saluted her with patriotic songs.

"The First Martyr" tells the story of a visit to the wife of John Brown before the latter's execution:

My five-years' darling, on my knee,

Chattered and toyed and laughed with me;

"Now tell me, mother mine," quoth she,

"Where you went i' the afternoon."

"Alas! my pretty little life,

I went to see a sorrowing wife,

Who will be widowed soon."

Child! It is fit that thou shouldst weep;

The very babe unborn would leap

To rescue such as he.

"Our Country" contains no word about the civil strife, although it is classed with "Poems of the War" in her volume entitled *Later Lyrics*. A prize was offered for a national song while the war was in progress, and Mrs. Howe sent in this poem, Otto Dresel composing the music. Mr. Dresel was a prominent figure in the musical world of Boston for many years and wrote a number of charming songs.

The prize which had been offered for the national song was never awarded, if I remember aright, and Mr. Dresel decided to use the tune he had composed, for the "Army Hymn" of Oliver Wendell Holmes. This was "superbly sung by L. C. Campbell, assisted by the choir and band" at the opening exercises of the Great Metropolitan Fair held in New York during the Civil War, for the benefit of the Sanitary Commission.

"Our Country" thus lost its musical setting, to my mother's regret.

OUR COUNTRY

On primal rocks she wrote her name,

Her towers were reared on holy graves,

The golden seed that bore her came

Swift-winged with prayer o'er ocean waves.

The Forest bowed his solemn crest,

And open flung his sylvan doors;

Meek Rivers led the appointed Guest

To clasp the wide-embracing shores;

Till, fold by fold, the broidered Land
To swell her virgin vestments grew,
While Sages, strong in heart and hand,
Her virtue's fiery girdle drew.

O Exile of the wrath of Kings!
O Pilgrim Ark of Liberty!
The refuge of divinest things,
Their record must abide in thee.

First in the glories of thy front
Let the crown jewel Truth be found;
Thy right hand fling with generous wont
Love's happy chain to furthest bound.

Let Justice with the faultless scales
Hold fast the worship of thy sons,
Thy commerce spread her shining sails
Where no dark tide of rapine runs.

So link thy ways to those of God,
So follow firm the heavenly laws,
That stars may greet thee, warrior-browed,
And storm-sped angels hail thy cause.

O Land, the measure of our prayers,
Hope of the world, in grief and wrong!
Be thine the blessing of the years,
The gift of faith, the crown of song.

The news of Lincoln's assassination dealt a stunning blow to our people. The rejoicings over the end of the Civil War were suddenly changed to deep sorrow, indignation, and fear. How widely the conspiracy spread we did not know. It will be remembered that other officers of the Federal Government were attacked. My mother wrote that nothing since the death of her little boy[40] had given her so much personal pain. As usual, she sought relief for her feelings in verse. "The Parricide," written on the day of Lincoln's funeral, expresses her love and reverence for the great man, her horror of the "Fair assassin, murder—white," whom she bids:

With thy serpent speed avoid

Each unsullied household light,

Every conscience unalloyed.

As usual, compassion followed anger. "Pardon," written a few days later, after the death of Wilkes Booth, is the better poem of the two.

PARDON

WILKES BOOTH—APRIL 26, 1865

Pains the sharp sentence the heart in whose wrath it was uttered,

Now thou art cold;

Vengeance, the headlong, and Justice, with purpose close muttered,

Loosen their hold.

Death brings atonement; he did that whereof ye accuse him,—

Murder accurst;

But, from that crisis of crime in which Satan did lose him,

Suffered the worst.

Back to the cross, where the Saviour uplifted in dying

Bade all souls live,

Turns the reft bosom of Nature, his mother, low sighing,

Greatest, forgive!

On July 21, 1865, Harvard University held memorial exercises in honor of her sons who had given their lives for their country. The living graduates of that day numbered only twenty-four hundred, including the aged, sick, and absent. Of these more than five hundred went out to fight in behalf of the Union, many of them to return no more. Their names may be seen engraved on the marble tablets of Memorial Hall, Cambridge, a daily lesson in patriotism to the undergraduates who frequent it. Full of fun and nonsense as the latter are, they will permit no disrespect to the memory of the heroes of the Civil War. If visitors enter without removing their hats, an instant clamor arises, forcing them to do so.

On this Commencement day of 1865 a notable assemblage gathered at Harvard. In addition to other distinguished people there were present, as Governor Andrew said in his address, a "cloud of living witnesses who have come back laden with glory from the fields where their comrades fell." Phillips Brooks made a prayer, Ralph Waldo Emerson and others spoke. Oliver Wendell Holmes, Rev. Charles T. Brooks, James Russell Lowell, his brother Robert, John S. Dwight, and Mrs. Julia Ward Howe contributed poems. The verses of the latter were read by her friend, Mr. Samuel Eliot. The opening ones are as follows:

RETURN

They are coming, oh my Brothers, they are coming!

From the formless distance creeps the growing sound,

Like a rill-fed forest, in whose rapid summing,

Stream doth follow stream, till waves of joy abound.

These have languished in the shadow of the prison,

Long with hunger pains and bitter fever low;

Welcome back our lost, from living graves arisen,

From the wild despite and malice of the foe.

Another of her war poems speaks in the name of the sons of the old university. When it was published in the newspapers, a careless typesetter made some errors in setting it up. I remember how troubled she was when the line

O give them back, thou bloody breast of Treason—

was printed "beast" of Treason.

We give a single verse of the "Harvard Student's Song":

Remember ye how, out of boyhood leaping,

Our gallant mates stood ready for the fray,

As new-fledged eaglets rise, with sudden sweeping,

And meet unscared the dazzling front of day?

Our classic toil became inglorious leisure,

We praised the calm Horatian ode no more,

But answered back with song the martial measure,

That held its throb above the cannon's roar.

The other "Poems of the War" published in *Later Lyrics* are entitled "Requital," "The Question," "One and Many," "Hymn for a Spring Festival," "The Jeweller's Shop in War-time," and "The Battle Eucharist."

In these we see how deeply the writer's soul was oppressed by the sorrow of the war and the horrors of the battle-field. We see, too, how it turned ever for comfort and encouragement to the Cross and to the Lord of Hosts.

X
MRS. HOWE'S LOVE OF FREEDOM AN INHERITANCE

Stories of Gen. Francis Marion—Mrs. Howe's kinship with the "Swamp Fox"—The episode that saved "Marion's Men"—The splendid sword that rusted in its scabbard—John Ward, one of Oliver Cromwell's Ironsides—Samuel Ward, the only Colonial governor who refused to enforce the Stamp Act—Roger Williams, founder of Rhode Island and champion of religious liberty.

WE have seen that my mother's love of freedom was in part the result of environment. It was also an inheritance from men who had fought for civil and religious liberty, with the sword and with the pen, on both sides of the Atlantic. Of the founder of the Ward family in America, we know that he fought for the English Commonwealth and against "Charles First, tyrant of England." He was one of Oliver Cromwell's Ironsides, serving as an officer in a cavalry regiment. After the republic perished and the Stuart line in the person of Charles II. returned to the throne, doughty old John Ward came to America, bringing his good sword with him. Whether it was ever used on this side of the water, the record does not say, but it was preserved in the family for nearly a century.

His descendants held positions of trust and responsibility under the State, his grandson and great-grandson being each in his turn governor of Rhode Island. The latter, Gov. Samuel Ward, has the distinction of being the only Colonial governor who refused to take the oath to enforce the Stamp Act. As the Chief Executive of "little Rhody" was chosen by the people, his views were naturally more democratic than those of governors appointed by the crown. Still, it took courage to refuse to obey the royal mandate. He early foresaw the separation from Great Britain and wrote to his son in 1766, "These Colonies are destined to an early independence, and you will live to see my words verified." He was a member of the Continental Congresses of 1774 and 1775. The latter resolved itself into a committee of the whole almost every day, and Governor Ward was constantly called to the chair on such occasions, until he was seized with fatal illness, March 13, 1776, dying soon afterward.

At this time vaccination had not been discovered, the only preventive of the terrible scourge of smallpox being inoculation. Now Governor Ward could not spare time for the brief illness which this process involved. In addition to his duties in Congress he was obliged, owing to the physical disability of his colleague, Gov. Stephen Hopkins, to conduct all the official correspondence of the Rhode Island delegation, with the Government and citizens of the colony. His services were required on many committees, notably on the secret committee which contracted for arms and munitions of war. Hence, worn down by overwork, he fell an easy victim to smallpox. He died three months before his colleagues signed the Declaration of Independence. As he early saw the necessity of separation from the mother country, he would certainly have affixed his signature to it had he lived. His descendants may be pardoned for thinking that he made a great mistake in not taking the time required for inoculation.

Many of Governor Ward's letters have been preserved. These show his ardent patriotism as well as the devout religious spirit of the men of 1776. He writes to his brother: "I have realized with regard to myself the bullet, the bayonet, and the halter; and compared with the immense object I have in view they are all less than nothing. No man living, perhaps, is more fond of his children than I am, and I am not so old as to be tired of life; and yet, as far as I can now judge, the tenderest connections and the most important private concerns are very minute objects. Heaven save my country! I was going to say is my first, my last, and almost my only prayer."

Gov. Samuel Ward was a Seventh-Day Baptist. The little church in which he worshiped at Newport has all the charm of the best architecture of that period. It now forms part of the Historical Society's rooms.

His son, Lieut.-Col. Samuel Ward, grandfather of Mrs. Julia Ward Howe, joined the Continental Army when the Revolution broke out. Governor Ward writes of "the almost unparalleled sufferings of Samuel," and these were indeed severe. Of the ill-fated expedition to Quebec, Colonel Ward writes: "We were thirty days in a wilderness that none but savages ever attempted to pass. We marched one hundred miles upon shore with only three days' provisions, waded over three rapid rivers, marched through snow and ice barefoot ... moderately speaking, we have waded one hundred miles." The result of this exposure was "the yellow jaundice."

The Americans were overpowered by superior numbers, Colonel Ward being taken prisoner with many others. He was also at Valley Forge in that terrible winter when the American Army endured such great privations.

It is interesting to note that Colonel Ward assisted in raising a colored regiment in the spring of 1778. He commanded this in the engagement on the island of Rhode Island, near the spot where his granddaughter and her husband established their summer home a century later. From the peaceful windows of "Oak Glen" one sees, in the near foreground, the earthworks of the Revolution.

In spite of all the hardships endured during the Revolutionary War, Colonel Ward lived to be nearly seventy-six years of age. My mother well remembered her grandfather with his courtly manner and mild, but very observing, blue eyes. With the indulgence characteristic of grandparents, he permitted the Ward brothers to play cards at his house, a thing they were forbidden to do at home.

The State of Rhode Island is represented in the statue-gallery of the national Capitol by Roger Williams, pioneer of religious liberty and founder of the State, and by Gen. Nathaniel Greene, who rendered such important service during the Revolutionary War. My mother was related to both men, being a direct descendant of the former.

Whether or no Massachusetts was justified in driving out Roger Williams, we will not attempt to decide. He was evidently a person who delighted in controversy in a day when religious toleration was almost unknown.

To him belongs the honor of being the first to found a State "upon the distinctive principle of complete separation of Church and State." Maryland followed not long after the example set by the "State of Rhode Island and Providence Plantations."

Not in Massachusetts alone did people object to his doctrines. His work, *The Bloody Tenent of Persecution*, was burned in England by the common hangman, by order of Parliament.

George Fox Digged Out of His Burrowe seems a volume of formidable proportions to the modern reader. With Quaker doctrines Roger Williams had small patience, although he permitted members of the persecuted sect to live in the Colony. It seems that G. Fox did not avail himself of an offer of disputation on fourteen proposals. His opponents claimed that he "slily departed" to avoid the debate. It went on just the same, being "managed three days at Newport and one day at Providence."

This volume, *George Fox*, etc.[41], is dedicated to Charles II. by "Your Majestyes most loyal and affectionate Orator at the Throne of Grace."

One can guess how much attention the Merrie Monarch paid to the fourteen "proposalls"[42] and the elaboration thereof.

The best testimony to the essential gentleness and goodness of this eccentric divine is the behavior toward him of the Indians. During King Philip's war they marched on Providence with the intention of burning it.

"The well-attested tradition is that Roger Williams, now an old man, alone and unarmed, save with his staff, went out to meet the band of approaching Indians. His efforts to stay their course were unavailing, but they allowed him to return unmolested, such was the love and veneration entertained for him by these savages."

Of my mother's ancestors on the maternal side, the most interesting was her great-great-uncle, Gen. Francis Marion, the partisan leader of the Revolution. She was descended from his sister Esther, "The Queen Bee of the Marion Hive," the general himself having no children.

Many romantic stories are told of him. He was present at a drinking-party during the siege of Charleston when the host, determined that no one should leave the festivities until some particularly fine Madeira had been disposed of, locked the door and threw the key out of the window. Marion had no notion of taking part in any excesses, so he made his escape by jumping out of the window. A lame ankle was the result, and the Huguenot left the city, all officers unfit for duty being ordered to depart. Marion took refuge now with one friend, now with another, and again he was obliged to hide in the woods, while recovering from this lameness. The accident was a most fortunate one, however. If he had remained in Charleston he would have been obliged to surrender and the brigade of "Marion's Men" might never have existed.

How he formed it in the darkest hour of the war in the South is a matter of history. How, like so many will-o'-the-wisps, they led the British a weary dance "thoro' bush, thoro' brier," all through the woods and the swamps of South Carolina, is a tale that delights the heart of every school-boy.

Well knows the fair and friendly moon

The men that Marion leads,

The glitter of the rifles,

The scamper of their steeds;

'Tis life to guide the fiery barb

Across the moonlit plain:

'Tis life to feel the night-wind

That lifts the tossing mane.

A moment in the British camp,

A moment and away,

Back to the pathless forest

Before the peep of day.[43]

The best-known story tells of the British officer who was brought blindfolded into Marion's camp and entertained at a dinner consisting solely of sweet potatoes. Small wonder that he made up his mind the Americans could not be conquered, since they were able to subsist on such scanty rations!

Reversing the text of Scripture, General Marion provided his men with swords made of saws, ammunition being scanty. He was as well known for his humanity as for his ingenuity. It is said that once, wishing to draw his sword, he found it rusted into the scabbard, so little had it been used.

When my mother, as occasionally happened in her later years, would quietly slip off on some expedition which her daughters feared was too much for her strength, we would remember her kinship with the "Swamp Fox."

Of her parents, it should be said that both were deeply religious. Her mother, Julia Cutler Ward, a woman of very lovely character and intellectual tastes, died at the early age of twenty-seven. Her father, Samuel Ward, one of the "Merchant Princes of Wall Street," was well known for his integrity, liberality, and public spirit. He was especially interested in the causes of temperance and religion, being "one of the foremost promoters of church-building in the then distant West." He was also one of the founders of the New York University, and owned the first private picture-gallery in New York.

Thus we see that my mother, like so many of her fellow-Americans, came from a long line of God-fearing and patriotic men and women. In the words of the "Battle Hymn" we hear not only the voice of the Union Army, but an echo of all the aspiring thoughts and noble deeds of the builders of our great Republic.

THE END

FOOTNOTES:

[1] Abraham Lincoln said of this law: "I look upon that enactment not as a law, but as a violence from the beginning. It was conceived in violence and is being executed in violence" (letter to Joshua F. Speed, August 24, 1855).

[2] From *The Journals and Letters of Samuel Gridley Howe*. Dana, Estes & Co.

[3] "Chev" was the abbreviation of Chevalier, a title bestowed on him for his services in the Greek Revolution. He was called "Chev" by certain intimate friends.

[4] The Kansas and Nebraska bill.

[5] Protesting against the Missouri Compromise.

[6] From *Reminiscences* by Julia Ward Howe. Houghton, Mifflin & Co.

[7] *Recollections of the Anti-Slavery Struggle*. By Julia Ward Howe.

[8] *Ibid.*

[9] Letter from Dr. S. G. Howe to Charles Sumner.

[10] *Journals and Letters of Samuel Gridley Howe*. Dana, Estes & Co.

[11] History declares that a colleague of Brooks did thus stand, to prevent any one's coming to Sumner's assistance. About the pistols, I am not sure.

[12] Sketch of John Albion Andrew by Eben F. Stone.

[13] *Recollections of the Anti-Slavery Struggle*. By Julia Ward Howe.

[14] *Reminiscences* by Julia Ward Howe.

[15] *Ibid.*

[16] *Ibid.*

[17] From *Journals and Letters of Samuel Gridley Howe*. Dana, Estes & Co.

[18] *Reminiscences.*

[19] *Ibid.*

[20] *Ibid.*

[21] *Ibid.*

[22] See Chap. ii, page 33.

[23] *Recollections of the Anti-Slavery Struggle.*

[24] *Reminiscences*, 1899.

[25] In the reprint of the "Battle Hymn," made in England for the use of the soldiers during the present war, this discarded verse has, through some misunderstanding, been included.

[26] See *Julia Ward Howe*, Vol. II, Chap. xi.

[27] This account of the day in Libby Prison is compiled from the *Washington Star* and from the *Life of Chaplain McCabe*.

[28] *Life of Chaplain McCabe*.

[29] *Ibid.*

[30] *Reminiscences* by Julia Ward Howe.

[31] *Julia Ward Howe*. By Laura E. Richards and Maud Howe Elliott.

[32] *Life of Julia Ward Howe*.

[33] See Chapter IX.

[34] In the later editions of the novel another scene is substituted for this.

[35] *Life of Chaplain McCabe*—"the singing chaplain."

[36] *Julia Ward Howe*. Houghton, Mifflin & Co.

[37] Mr. Howells writes in his *Literary Boston Thirty Years Ago*: "I heard Mrs. Howe speak in public and it seemed to me that she made one of the best speeches I had ever heard."

[38] *Reminiscences*, p. 261.

[39] *Ibid.*, p. 258.

[40] Samuel Gridley Howe, Jr., who died in May, 1863, aged three and a half years.

[41] *George Fox Digged Out of His Burrowe*.

[42] "Proposalls"—I here quote Roger Williams' spelling.

[43] William Cullen Bryant's "The Song of Marion's Men."

Milton Keynes UK
Ingram Content Group UK Ltd.
UKHW030846141124
451205UK00005B/462